Heidi Garrett

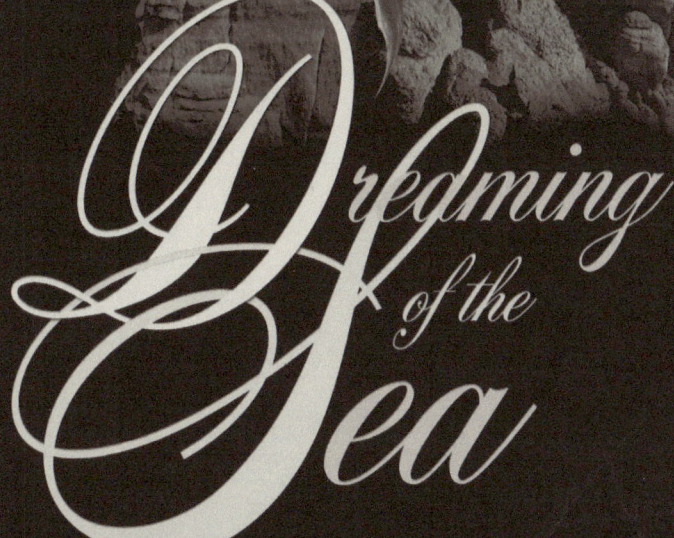

Dreaming *of the* Sea

A CONTEMPORARY FAIRY TALE

Other Books by Heidi Garrett

Sign up for Heidi's newsletter!
http://eepurl.com/wWKUj

Daughter of Light

(A Young Adult Fantasy Trilogy)

Isolt's Enchantment, A Prequel
Half Faerie, #1
Half Mortal, #2
War & Grace, #3

Once Upon a Time Today

(A Collection of Stand-Alone Modern Fairy Tale Retellings)

The Girl Who Believed in Fairy Tales: Three Short Stories
Beautiful Beautiful
The Tree Hugger
I Am Lily Dane

In Collaboration with Billie Limpin

(A New Adult Paranormal Romance)

Cupcakes and Kisses

To Norma Elder

Who believed in prayer

Contents

Part I: Orphans

2005 –

Nine-year-old Miriam clutched her pink sock monkey as she stared at the television. Perched on the edge of the sofa, because she could never properly balance in the enormous and uncomfortable dip in its middle, she ran her tongue over the ridges of her chapped lower lip. When she found a bit of loose skin she chewed it off. It was impossible to concentrate on what Ernie and the Cookie Monster were saying. The escalating grunts and murmurs coming from the apartment's single bedroom split her attention, even though the door was closed.

It was winter, and the apartment was cold. As the sun set, the temperature inside became frigid. Miriam's oversized sweats and thin t-shirt offered little warmth as the living room darkened. Her mother often turned off the heat to save money. Miriam rubbed her eyes. The two hours of Sesame Street reruns were almost finished. Her favorite show, My Little Pony, was next. Her stomach gurgled. She glanced at the closed bedroom door and strained her ears. They must be passed out. If she was lucky they'd remain that way until morning, and Miriam would be at school when the bedroom door finally opened.

Sometimes she got lucky.

The kitchen and living room were one space, separated by a counter. On the way to the pantry, Miriam carefully stepped around the squeaky spot beneath the stained carpet. Besides the ends of a loaf of bread in a knotted plastic sack, there wasn't much on the shelves. Jars of peanut butter, mustard, pickle relish, and a few cans of Campbell soup. A bowl of soup would warm her up, but she couldn't risk banging the pot against the stove. A peanut butter and jelly sandwich would have to do.

Dreaming of the Sea

Miriam reached for the bread and peanut butter. She set them down softly on the kitchen counter. She stood before the refrigerator and sucked in her breath. If she wasn't careful, the door would make a loud smack when it closed. Maybe she should forget the jelly.

She glanced back at the bedroom door. It remained safely closed. A peanut butter and jelly sandwich would taste so good. Miriam yanked on the refrigerator door. Light spilled out. It was as empty as the pantry, but there was a half-full jar of grape jelly on the side door. She eased it out. With her other hand, she gripped the door handle. When it was almost closed, she let go. It made a slight pop as it sealed. Miriam froze.

Her pulse pounded in her ears as she slowly turned. Miriam screamed and dropped the jar. It rolled across the floor until it banged against the bottom of the refrigerator.

The man her mother had brought home earlier leaned with his elbows against the counter, watching her. His long stringy hair reached past his shoulders. Miriam couldn't begin to count the number of tattoos on the threatening bare skin of his arms and chest.

She backed away as he came around the counter and picked up the jelly.

He pulled open the refrigerator and slid the jar next to a six-pack of beer. He crouched down in front of Miriam, who stood with her back against the wall. "You can have dinner after we play."

Miriam's stomach heaved. He took her hand. She refused to walk. He pulled harder. Her sock-covered feet slid.

"She doesn't want to come," he shouted to Miriam's mother.

Lights flicked on in the bedroom.

Once attractive, Helen now looked used up. Gaunt and sallow, a belt circled her bicep. She staggered toward the man and her daughter. "Hey, honey, don't you want to play fashion model?"

Miriam's eyes welled with tears. Fashion models wore clothes.

§§§

The 1500s –

Once upon a time, a woman tempted to throw herself from a seaside cliff onto the killing rocks below paused to reconsider: Would it be more satisfying if her lover could feel the agony that ripped her heart to shreds and pulverized its remaining tissue with meaty blows? Yes, she thought. Revenge would be more sweet than immolation.

Her plea, so genuine and determined, reached the devil's ear. It was just the kind of dilemma he relished.

When he arrived on the blustery promontory, he paid his compliments. "In the throes of devastating betrayal, few have the presence of mind to stop and think. Yet how much more satisfying than suicide is an eye for an eye—a tooth for a tooth— a heart for a heart."

The woman seethed. She dug her fingernails into her palms, drawing blood. The devil caught a whiff. He encouraged her to confide her tale.

"The man I believed mine—" The woman banged her wounded hand against her breast. Two drops of blood speckled the front of her simple dress. She broke down, hiccoughing, before she wiped her tears away, leaving a smear of blood from her cheek to her chin. "He's a sailor. His easy lies concealed wives, lovers, and children. He abandons them in every port like stray dogs. I found proof in a wooden chest he keeps locked away in his boat. Oh, he denied it all, until I shoved those love letters and trinkets down his throat." She laughed, it was a gash to the ears. "After he choked them up, he gloated over my naiveté. 'Did you think you were the only one?'" The woman moaned.

"I know of a volcano," the devil said, for he'd contrived an elegant solution.

The woman listened with every pore.

"It's at the bottom of the sea and needs tending."

"What kind of care does a volcano require, especially one on the ocean floor?"

"It would be better if it had some kind of guardian," the devil's tone was matter-of-fact; it always was when ploughing the ground for the purchase of a soul. "A witch is what I'm thinking," he said.

"What kind of a witch?"

"A sea witch."

"And how will that suit my need for revenge?"

"Oh, it will suit your need very well. I'll grant you the ability to draw from the volcano's raw power. In its proximity, you'll control the very sea. And it's not far from here." The devil pointed to the cove. "Your man, does he sail these waters with some frequency?" He drew a square in the air between the visible shore and the sea's horizon.

"Yes, his routes are most commonly in these waters."

"Then you might conjure a sea storm, and when his wrecked

ship sinks to the ocean floor, you could salvage his bones. Make some little knickknacks with them."

"Where would I keep them?"

The devil stroked his goatee, for he'd chosen an urbane facade. "You would need a lair, I think. A place of your own, in the volcano's shadow."

"But I can't live underwater!"

"Ah." The devil clasped his hands behind his back. The movement pulled open his grey tweed jacket and exposed his fine white shirt, satin vest, and the gold chain of a pocket watch. He liked to attend to details when he made these appearances. "I've forgotten to mention the best part haven't I?" The woman's puzzled expression encouraged him. She would agree to the pact, he was certain. "There are creatures who inhabit the sea–light-filled vermin who sing and celebrate all the time. They're rather annoying in their banality." He sniffed. "Perhaps you've heard of them. They're called mermaids."

"Oh, they're nothing but storybook creatures–they're not real."

"I assure you they are." The devil put his hands in his pockets and made a half-turn. "Walk with me."

7

She followed along beside him.

"Let's say, you're not only the volcano's custodian, but you're also given the power to take and restore the ability to live in the sea." He paused his stride. "You could take a mermaid's fins and replace them with legs. Or you could take a mortal's legs and replace them with fins." He released his chin and waved a hand in the air. "Of course, you'd have the talent for the usual spells and draughts too. "

The woman held up her hand and ticked off the devil's promises. "Keeper of the volcano, ability to create sea storms, giver and taker of fins and legs, talent for spells and draughts, plus my own little cottage on the ocean floor."

"Yes, yes, of course."

It all sounded to good to be true. "You'll be wanting something from me, I suppose."

"Only your soul."

The woman wasn't the god-fearing type; she wasn't even convinced she had a soul. "That's all, my soul?"

"With the many powers I'm bestowing upon you, and given the blackness roiling in your heart, I imagine you'll be up to all sorts of no good. You don't want to have to pay for all that in the afterlife, do you?"

The woman snorted. "Of course not."

"Didn't think so. The day you die, I'll harvest your soul and leave you to slumber peacefully through eternity."

The woman liked to sleep. "And if you don't take my soul? What will happen to me then?"

"That will depend on the the quality of your choices while you're alive."

"Then it's true, all that stuff about heaven and hell," the woman murmured. Being no saint, she hated to think of the crimes she might already be spiritually indebted for.

"Very true."

"Maybe it's better if I don't—"

"Have to take responsibility for any of your actions."

"Exactly." She considered his proposition a bit more and realized she'd come out on top. "I don't know why more folks don't deal directly with you."

"It's a mystery to me as well." The devil chuckled. "There is one more small matter."

The woman's fantasies of extracting vengeance from her lover came to a halt. What more could there be?

"It would be splendid if you could locate an apprentice who'll take your place before you die," the devil said. "In fact, I think I'll make that part of the contract."

The woman plucked at her dress. "But how will I find one?"

The devil gave her question some thought. "I see your point. It would be hard, if not impossible, to convince one of those simpering mermaids to take your place. Perhaps you should be amphibious," he mused.

"What does that mean?"

"You'll be able to walk on land and swim in the sea. You'll be the only one who can."

"You mean I'll have legs when I'm not in the water?"

"Yes, and fins when you're in the sea. Rather ingenious, don't you think? It will make it much easier to find a mortal to serve as your apprentice."

"Oh, all right. I suppose that's not too much to ask."

"I thought not."

And so, the first sea witch in a long line of sea witches came into being.

§§§

1852 –

Nine-year-old Gertrude lazed on a pile of rubble outside the sea witch's lair. The stack of rotting clothes, disintegrating maps, and swathes of decomposing canvas, which had once

10

waved in sea breezes and snapped in crosswinds as proud sails, overflowed a warped crate re-shaped to Gertrude's body. The make-shift couch was the sea witch's apprentice preferred spot to kill time.

In the depths of her lair, Beulah, gulped and sputtered. The sea witch was a noisy sleeper. At least she wasn't nagging Gertrude to collect fecal pellets, fungi, sea urchin spines, or worms this afternoon. Gertrude chewed on a thumbnail. No matter how assiduously she gnawed the thick, gray thing, it never broke or splintered. In her peripheral vision, the snake-like coils of her hair writhed as if they were alive. She did her best to ignore them as she passed some gas. As usual, she'd eaten too much mush.

Beulah boiled water spiders, water snakes, and water bugs over kettles of lava extracted from the nearby volcano. The tasty stew was the only thing about being the sea witch's apprentice that Gertrude liked, and she always ate too much of it.

She shifted on the mound of trash as another puff of wind escaped her blob-shaped body. Her gaze followed the yellow-green cloud until it collided with a glimmer of light. What's this? Gertrude pushed herself up onto her wrists.

The glow swam in her direction. It haloed a creature unlike any Gertrude had ever seen. Her eyes widened at the sight of the silky golden hair, creamy complexion, and graceful tail fin covered in a mosaic of shimmering scales.

"Are you the sea witch?" the creature trilled.

Gertrude gaped and shook her head.

"Do you know where she lives?"

Gertrude pointed to the dark opening behind her. "What are you?" she asked the creature in her rough voice.

"A mermaid."

"I'll tell Beulah you're here."

"Thank you." The mermaid twirled her slim hands in graceful spirals, treading water.

"Beulah!" Gertrude yelled. Her eyes remained on the mermaid's pearly fingernails.

"What are you yapping about now?" Beulah grumbled from the lair's interior.

"Are you here for a spell?" Gertrude tried to soften her voice, but it came out more like a hiss.

The mermaid arched backward as she nodded.

"Customer!" Gertrude yelled. "Go on inside."

The mermaid hesitated before swishing her sparkly tail to

propel her into the depths of the sea witch's lair.

Inside, Beulah sat on her own throne of trash. "Well, what do you want?"

"I need legs–human ones. I've been told you have the power to–" The mermaid's graceful tail went limp under the gaze of Beulah's beady eyes. "Grant my wish."

"I don't grant anything." Beulah ran her finger over a pile of bottles filled with rays of fluorescent gold, blue, green, and pink. "My potions and spells are costly."

Gertrude thought the mermaid's eyes watered. Although, at the bottom of the sea, it was always hard to tell.

"I don't have any gold."

"No? That's too bad."

"I must have a pair of human legs." The mermaid's hands fluttered to her chest. "I've fallen in love."

"Of course you have," Beulah snickered. "Do you have anything of value?"

The mermaid blinked her blue eyes. "Why, I don't know."

Beulah grunted. "If you can't pay for the potion, you won't be getting any legs."

Gertrude watched the exchange with increasing interest. "Do you have any jewelry?"

The mermaid gave her head a sorrowful shake.

"Maybe you know where a treasure chest is buried?" Gertrude prompted, although she wasn't exactly sure why she wanted to help the mermaid.

"No," the mermaid whispered.

"Then go on. Get of here." Beulah waved her lumpy arms.

"I can sing," the mermaid said. "I've been told I have a beautiful voice."

Beulah's brow creased. "Let me hear a song."

The mermaid closed her eyes and clasped her hands. Even though her sweet-sounding voice quavered and trembled, it was a delicate and alluring sound.

When she was finished singing, Beulah's eyes narrowed. "I'll trade your voice for a pair of legs."

The mermaid agreed.

"You understand you won't ever be able to speak again, and every time you take a step on those human legs it's going to feel like you're walking on a pair of knives."

Gertrude thought the mermaid's eyes were tearing up again, even as she clung to the bargain.

"All trades are final. There's no taking it back if your human doesn't return your love."

The mermaid fluttered her eyelashes. "I understand."

"Well, then."

Gertrude hovered nearby as the sea witch boiled some worms and crab eyes.

Beulah tossed two handfuls of smashed snail shells into the pot as she muttered an incantation. At the last minute the sea witch whipped out her free hand to catch a handful of her apprentice's skirt. "Bring me the yellow one and the blue one." The sea witch pointed to the coral-colored vials on the shelf of bones.

Gertrude obeyed.

Beulah stirred all of the yellow elixir and half of the blue into the pot before refilling each vial with the bubbling ingredients. Now, the liquid in the first vial was a muddy brown and the liquid in the second was a deep, slimy green. Beulah gave the muddy brown potion to the mermaid. "It will scrape your throat going down, but when it comes back up it will bring your voice with it."

The mermaid's pale skin turned paler.

"Get the bucket," Beulah ordered Gertrude. When her apprentice had the rusted pail in hand, the sea witch told the mermaid to drink up.

15

She did.

"Every last drop," Beulah croaked.

The drained vial slipped from the mermaid's fingers. Her lips pursed, her eyes rolled, she clutched her throat, her entire body convulsed.

Gertrude couldn't believe anyone would willingly undergo such treatment for anything.

When the mermaid began to choke, Beulah shoved the swamp green vial at Gertrude at the same time she grabbed the bucket from her. "Don't just stand there like an idiot. You have to catch her voice!"

A radiant spittle erupted from the mermaid's small mouth.

Beulah captured every drop. Her black eyes shined with glee.

When the mermaid opened her mouth, she winced. No sound came out.

"Your throat is raw. It will heal in time. But you'll never speak or sing again." Beulah cackled.

For the first time Gertrude truly contemplated the power that would someday be hers.

Beulah told her apprentice to give the mermaid the second potion. "Don't take it until you're on land. Otherwise you might drown." The sea witch cackled again. "It's going to feel like someone is sawing off your tail fin and nailing legs in its place. But maybe your human will return your love, and it will all be worth it."

The mermaid's eyes remained downcast as she draped the vial's chain around her neck then hurriedly exited the lair.

Gertrude was full of questions. "Why are we so ugly?"

"Witches must be fierce creatures." The sea witch nodded toward the retreating mermaid. "Who would be afraid of her?"

"Maybe fear isn't the only kind of power. Did you see how even the eels stopped to look at her?"

Beulah whacked Gertrude on the side of the head. "Be grateful for what you've got." The sea witch smashed a handful of poached sea beetles into her mouth. "There's lots of girls who'd be glad to take your place. Your mother did you a favor by bringing you to me early on. You've got lots of time to study and develop your cunning. By the time I'm gone, you'll be one of the most powerful sea witches who ever lived."

Gertrude never liked to be reminded of her mother who'd traded her to the sea witch for a love potion when Gertrude was still an infant. "It would be easier to understand why the mermaid wanted to trade her tail fin if she had a black snake tail

17

like you and me."

Beulah cuffed her again. "Nothing is wrong with our tails, girl."

The back of Gertrude's head smarted.

"If you ask me, that mermaid is stupid," Beulah squawked.

"What are you going to do with her voice?"

"Hoard it." Beulah gave Gertrude's ear a painful tweak. "I don't like to let go of anything. You never know when it might come in handy."

"Have you ever been on land?" Gertrude asked her mentor.

"Last time I went up there, I got you. I don't want for anything else. Taking trips is a waste of time if you ask me. Home sweet home is my motto."

Gertrude fell silent. Beulah, often exhausted after working magic, spread out on a trough of bones.

When the sea witch began to snore, her apprentice swam after the mermaid. Hiding in the shadows, Gertrude tried to catch up with the mesmerizing creature.

By the time Gertrude reached the border of their waters, the mermaid's light had receded to a faint flicker overhead.

Gertrude watched the slim ray of light as it continued to ascend. After it disappeared, she began to wonder: If her hair was smooth and flowing, not snake-like; if her complexion was fair, not pocked and scarred; if her form was comely, not in the shape of a blob with crooked hands and teeth protruding, would she be more powerful than Beulah?

It set Gertrude to dreaming.

§§§

The guy was probably older than Miriam, although not by much. A year or two, that would put him at about sixteen or seventeen. He was clean-shaven with short hair and didn't smell too bad. He was cleaning up somewhere. She wanted to find out where. The tolerance of the clerks at the 7-11 where the crew was currently taking hand baths was wearing thin. They would need to move on soon.

Freddy, Lucy, and Marta were already edging away. Probably, because the guy with the short hair was flinging his arms and shouting, not really to anyone, but pretty loud.

"What's your name?" Miriam asked.

Short Hair froze. He faced her with a mean squint. She took a step back. He took a menacing lunge in her direction. Miriam had been on the street for thirteen months. Pretty much since she and her mother had been evicted from their one bedroom apartment above the music store. When Helen

19

had landed in a dope house, her daughter had run away.

The streets were hard. Harder than Miriam had anticipated. But Miriam had always been good with the crazies. She had a calm demeanor—after everything she'd experienced in the first fifteen years of her life, little fazed her—and often sought to ease the isolation of troubled souls who everyone else shrank away from in fear and/or disgust.

She bobbed her head. "You don't have to tell me your name —"

He rushed her, his elbow in the air, his hand in the shape of a gun with two fingers pointed at the ground. "Stop staring at me!"

Miriam averted her eyes. He was right up in her face now. She could smell the beer on his breath. She scanned the park. It had emptied quickly. Most street people didn't want to fight. Lingering cuts and bruises, sometimes broken bones, slowed you down, distracted you, and generally increased your vulnerability.

As the guy's breath hit her cheek, she had to admit she'd made a mistake engaging him. She held up her hands in surrender. "Sorry. It's just...you're so clean...I was wondering where you're taking showers."

He banged the side of her head with his face.

"What is wrong with you?" Miriam ducked.

The angled tip of his duct-taped cowboy boot caught her chin. Her head flopped back and she lost her balance. He stomped down on her abdomen with the heel of his boot. She groaned.

"Don't even try to move in on my setup," he said.

She rolled to her side and curled in a fetal position to protect herself. Another strong kick connected with her back. Damned Freddy, Lucy, and Marta had abandoned her while this psycho pummeled her. He kept kicking. She was crying now. Begging him to stop in slobbery words. Finally, he did. He bent over and pulled her head up by the hair. "If you follow me, I'm going to kill you."

Like she could even walk.

He let her hair go so abruptly her skull slammed against the pavement. When he was gone, no one came to help her. Miriam stared up into the night sky at the only two stars visible in the city. Maybe it was time to at least check in with her mom.

Get off the street for a few days to figure things out.

§§§

The day Beulah died, the devil came to the sea witch's lair to retrieve her soul. Gertrude had a lot of questions.

To begin with, Beulah had never told her the devil looked like something that might have been born if a toadfish had mated with an eel. Frog Man, Gertrude called him in her mind. His bloated gills made his face square, and the prominent ridges that ran from the top of his head to the tip of his slick black tail were spiked with sharp needles. He waved a blood red square of silk beneath his nose. It exuded a scent that puzzled Gertrude. The nearest thing she could relate it to was the way their borders smelled after a particularly ferocious sea storm had wrecked a ship or two. Gertrude couldn't decide whether or not it was an improvement over the thick black odors that normally polluted the lair. She trailed close behind him anyway.

When he reached Beulah's bloated, heaving body, he paused to slip his handkerchief in one of the crepe-like folds of his skin. The sea witch was gasping and close to her last breath.

"How did you know when to come?" Gertrude asked him.

"I always know when it's time to collect a soul."

"So you'll know when to come for mine?"

"I will."

"It doesn't seem fair," Gertrude remarked.

The devil placed a smooth, inky black hand on Beulah's forehead and the other on her protruding stomach. He closed his eyes. "What doesn't seem fair?"

"Beulah chose this life for herself, but I didn't. My mum chose it for me. Shouldn't I get some kind of dispensation?"

The devil opened his eyes. He looked peeved, but he nodded.

"You agree?"

"Would it alleviate your sense of indignation to know that everyone I contract with feels the same way you do, at some point?"

"I'm not sure."

He held up a finger. "Let me finish my work here. Then I'll give you my undivided attention."

That pleased Gertrude. She settled down to watch.

He began to sing. The song sounded like a broken heart. Tears welled in her eyes. She blinked them away. Her heart swelled with a tender yearning, like a gorged river. "Why do I feel so sad when I'm not even particularly fond of Beulah?" she asked.

"Death is a great unifier. It always marks those who serve as its witness."

Gertrude pondered his answer. "Are you saying that when you're in the presence of death, it makes you feel connected?"

The devil bent over Beulah, placed his mouth over hers, pinched her nose, pressed hard on her belly, and closed his eyes again. His gills puffed out. His whole face expanded and contracted like a pair of bellows. Beulah's body shuddered. The devil pulled back, let go, and clapped his hands above his head five times. Then he swallowed. "There is no delicacy as grand as an immortal soul." He pulled out his blood red handkerchief and tapped the sides of his mouth. "Are you still feeling sad?"

Strangely, Gertrude's heartache had ended. "No."

"The Black Thorn Throne has passed to you."

Gertrude gazed around the lair. "That's great. I'll try to find it. I know it's around here somewhere, buried beneath the rubble."

"It's largely symbolic. My point is: The sea witch's crown is now yours. I trust Beulah prepared you for your duties."

"As far as I can tell."

"Then I'll leave it to you."

"That's it?"

"I'll come for your soul when it's time."

"Wait. Please!" Sometimes folks who came to the lair used that word *please* when they talked to Beulah. She'd told Gertrude it signaled they were desperate. "You can't just take Beulah's soul and leave me here all alone."

"I'm sorry. This appointment doesn't come with an instruction manual, and I'm not suited for friendship. Take heart. You have an obligation to apprentice the next witch."

"That's hardly a life." Gertrude sniffed. "Finding someone to replace me when I die."

The devil crossed his arms. "You'll have a long life, longer than if your mother hadn't traded you. You have magical powers. Take advantage. Enjoy!"

"I don't want to be left here, all alone."

The devil dabbed his brow with his handkerchief. "The sooner you find your apprentice, the sooner you'll gain a companion bound to you for the rest of your life. You'll never be alone again."

Gertrude rolled her neck and shoulders. For the first time in her life, she experienced a sensation of freedom. But she longed for something more.

The devil turned to leave.

"Wait!" she said.

He circled around. "Yes, Gertrude, what is it?"

"I'm amphibious?"

"Yes, all sea witches are. And?" He motioned for her to hurry up.

"How does that work? It's the one thing Beulah never taught me. She never left the lair."

"I see. Well, it's very straightforward. Swim to the water's surface and search for land. You can follow a ship or a bird. Once you reach the beach and remove yourself from the sea, your tail–" He pointed to it. "–will become a pair of human legs."

"And when I come back to the sea?"

"Simply soak your legs in salt water until your lovely tail has returned. Treading water is also an option."

"I don't understand why Beulah never took advantage of her amphibious nature."

"Each sea witch's proclivities are unique. But to me the distinctions are meaningless. Use your time and powers at your discretion. I won't intrude. My concerns are the fulfillment of the contract, its two specific points: Locating and training the next apprentice, and the willing gift of your immortal soul upon the day of your death. Adhere to those two points, and we won't have any problems."

§§§

Miriam took the stairs even though each step spiked the relentless pain in her ribs. She couldn't risk getting trapped in the elevator with some jacked up fiend when she was too injured to defend herself. The scent of urine and vomit polluted the dingy halls, and gang tags splattered every wall.

A guy with a knit cap sprawled on the 2nd floor landing. "Hey little lady, can you spare a twenty?"

Miriam's quick glance took in his high-priced neon sneakers. She gripped the straps of her backpack as she hustled by him. "Sorry."

"No worries," he mumbled.

Although it hurt to stand up straight—and breathe—she didn't stop moving until she reached apartment 312. The number three hung crooked. She knocked on the door. Not too hard, uncertain.

Nothing.

She knocked louder. Miriam pressed her ear against the

warped panel. Still no sound. She jiggled the knob. Not locked. "Mom," she called, as she slowly opened the door.

The apartment was bare, the TV and sofa probably pawned for brown.

"Mom." She winced as she slid her backpack off her shoulders and set it on the worn carpet. Miriam wrinkled her noise. The place smelled worse than the halls. A stained mattress with a wad of soiled sheets in its center was shoved in the corner. The room's single interior door stood halfway open. Miriam scanned the efficiency before heading toward the bathroom. A couple feet before she reached the threshold, she saw the bare feet tinged with blue-gray.

Her hand rose to cover her mouth. She spun and sagged against the wall. Miriam had seen enough dead bodies on the streets to know there was one in the bathroom of her mother's apartment. She slid down the wall. There was little doubt it was Helen.

Shit. Shit. Shit. What was she going to do now?

She cradled her head in her hands as her mind groped for options. Get the hell out of here. Return to the crew. They'd sacrificed her to save themselves and would do it again. She dropped her hand to the right side of her ribcage. The beating she'd taken last week had been a bad one. She rocked against the wall. Calling the police would lead to a lot of questions and another group home. She was too old to get fostered by a real family.

She crawled to the bathroom, bracing herself for what was coming.

Her mother stared at the ceiling. Dried vomit stained the side of her mouth, spilling into a gritty mustard-colored pool to the right of Helen's head. A rubber chord cinched her arm. The empty needle lay beside her hand. The bottom of a soda can lay less than a foot away, an afterthought on the cracked tile. The only thing she wore was a man's over-sized undershirt, grayed from too many washings.

Miriam covered Helen's body with one of the soiled sheets.

Then she stared out the apartment's single grimy window. There was a park across the street. A few guys were shooting hoops. If she opened the window, the dull throb from their boombox would rumble into the apartment and reverberate through her entire body. In the shadows, a guy—probably a dealer—checked his cellphone. A couple of girls, hugging textbooks to their chests, hurried through the park's center. Miriam recognized their hyper-vigilant postures.

The streets were exhausting.

Miriam returned to the dismal scene of her mother's last moments. She squatted and raised the sheet one last time. As she stared at the ruined face of the woman who'd given birth to her, she didn't feel much other than let down—again. The woman had been posting nude photos of her daughter online for almost fifteen years. Not a lot of love to be lost. Miriam let the sheet fall. She couldn't handle dealing with the body, but leaving Helen lying, half-dressed in her own vomit, didn't feel right either.

Miriam returned to her backpack, unzipped the side pocket, and pulled out the burner phone. After she dialed 9-1-1, she felt more in control. Not for the first time, she promised herself she would not end up like her mother.

When the police arrived, they sized up the neighborhood and Miriam's situation pretty quickly. They were direct but kind. They had to turn Miriam in to social services. It was the law. She knew this and didn't argue.

When the EMTs arrived, she asked to wait outside while they bagged Helen's body. After she signed some papers releasing her mother's body to be cremated, the older policeman asked if she was hungry. On the way to social services, they stopped by Five Guys to pick up a Double Cheeseburger, Cajun fries, and large Coke for her.

Miriam stuffed her pockets with peanuts while they waited for the order.

§§§

The mer king arrived a month after Beulah's death. Gertrude regarded him from a distance. He shined liked a streak of light, almost blinding her.

As he swam closer, she noted the whipped curve of his strong, gleaming tail, the wild tangle of his long golden hair, and the piercing gaze of his blue eyes.

She fancied the opportunity to test her sea witch skills on her first official customer. "What can I do for you?"

"My kingdom is under siege," he said. "The winter has been too long, and the sea grows colder every day. The mer people are a cold-blooded people. If the temperatures continue to drop, it will be the end of us."

She chewed on one of her scaly gray fingernails. "Sounds like that could be a problem."

He rubbed his biceps. Gertrude stared at the flexed muscles and caramel skin that contained them. It was so different from her own blotched gray hide. She longed to touch it. She reached out her hand. The mer king dodged. "It's cold in here, too. I thought your lair would be warmer, with its proximity to the volcano."

Gertrude dug her hands into the patched pockets of her dress—a burlap sack tied with twine into a sailor's knot. Beulah had salvaged it from the last wrecked ship they'd plundered. "Now that you mention it, it's a bit chillier than normal."

"Then, you've not traveled beyond your borders?"

"Busy." She indicated the lair. "Lots of work to do around here."

"The winter has been harsh," the mer king said. "The sea is freezing."

She'd learned from Beulah to never appear overeager to help. The more nonchalant she seemed, the harder the bargain she could strike. "I didn't know."

"If the ice encroaches, we're going to die," he continued.

Gertrude found a pinky bone and picked at the gaps between her teeth. "Everyone dies eventually."

"You're the sea witch," he said. "You have the power to save my kingdom!"

"Yes, that's true. I am the sea witch." Gertrude wanted to rub it in.

"Will you help me?"

"It will cost you."

"I have plenty of gold."

Gertrude pointed to the gold spilling from a chest in a corner of the lair. "So do I." She wished the mer king to suffer the price he paid. "Come closer," she instructed him.

Although he appeared to find her repugnant, he swam nearer. She pressed her hand to her brow and concentrated. What might a king value above all else? Her breath caught. Sons! Heirs! She opened one eye. What would she do with the mer king's sons if she had them? Swimming around her lair, interrupting her peace and quiet, that wouldn't do at all. No. She squeezed her eyes shut again and concentrated once more. But a single handsome mer prince at her beck and call would do nicely.

Her eyes popped open. "Give me your second son, and the second son of your first son, and the second son of his first son, and the second son of his first son—you get the idea, and we'll call it fair."

"I'll never agree to that."

Gertrude flounced on the nearest stack of bones. "Suit yourself. I'm not going to freeze to death."

"It's an exorbitant price. A payment so infinite, its value can't be measured."

Gertrude shrugged. "A single merman from each surviving generation or no surviving generations. Doesn't seem like such a hard choice to me."

The mer king swished back and forth, creating a whirlpool around himself. Customers often resorted to theatrics. Gertrude endured the spectacle with a practiced disinterest.

"My wife warned me against bargaining with you," he said.

"Is your wife going to save you, then?"

He pushed out his chest. Gorgeous pecs. "I won't pay your price."

Gertrude didn't say anything as she led him to the front of her lair. He would pay, eventually. They always did. She'd seen it time and time again with Beulah. No one came to the sea witch unless they'd exhausted their other options.

"I was generous!" she yelled as he swam away. "I could have asked for your first born." Beulah would have demanded his first born.

§§§

"Shut up!" the new girl towered over Miriam.

Four-year-old Amy's ear-piercing shrieks silenced everyone

in the dining hall.

"We don't steal food from kids," Miriam said.

The tall girl shoved her.

Miriam stumbled before regaining her stance. An older woman, Ruth entered her peripheral vision. The caseworker scooped up the hysterical Amy and marched toward Miriam and the new girl. Miriam said nothing, just stared at the yogurt pack in the new girl's hand. Amy's arms stretched out to take it back.

"Did you take that from Amy?" Ruth asked. Her voice was tight, angry but controlled.

The new girl shoved the container at the little girl. "Here's your stupid yogurt. It probably tastes like crap. Everything here does."

Ruth settled Amy at one of the tables. Miriam helped the little girl peel off the top of the yogurt container before going to stand in line with her lunch tray.

"Come with me," Ruth said to the new girl, who stormed out of the dining hall after the caseworker.

Miriam returned to sit next to Amy. The girl concentrated on her snack. When she was finished, she patted Miriam's leg. Amy never talked, only screamed or remained stubbornly mute.

Later that afternoon, in the caseworker's box of an office, Miriam perched on the edge of a chair with her elbows on Ruth's desk.

"I've found a permanent placement for you."

Tiny wings fluttered in Miriam's heart. "Where?"

"With the Sisters of Charity and Grace."

The bird soaring in Miriam's chest crash-landed. "A convent?"

"Life there will be quiet, orderly, and stable. You really need some stability."

"No men," Miriam whispered.

"None."

The bird hopped. "Safe," Miriam said.

"We've placed less than a handful of kids with them over the years. But every one of them has transitioned well into adulthood. It's a rare opportunity. The sisters provide a variety of training and skills. It will give you some choices about what you want to do with your life."

Happiness and sorrow made a tangled nest in Miriam's heart. "What will happen to Amy?"

"She's young. Her chances of getting a permanent family

are still good."

Miriam teared up. The toddler had crawled into her bed the first night she'd arrived at the group home two months ago. "I'll miss her."

Ruth reached across her desk to hold Miriam's hand. "That little girl is never going to forget you."

§ § §

When the mer king returned, Gertrude noticed that he wasn't chastened.

"We'll concede to your outrageous demands, witch, but not without protest."

"Pshaw!" Gertrude said. "Your protests are meaningless to me." She slid her thumb and forefinger in her mouth and made a sharp sound.

The king pressed his hands to his ears. "Stop that shrieking!"

"You heard that?" She never did.

"Of course, I heard it, I'm part fish."

Gertrude's gaze wandered over his sleek torso. The part that wasn't fish. What might it be like to touch that hairless chest, to allow her fingers to glide down all the way to where the taut skin melted into iridescent scales? She shivered.

The mer king's eyes narrowed. "Please don't tell me that you'll be molesting my son and the others."

Gertrude blinked and raised her gaze. "Molesting?"

"Using them as your personal toys, as playthings."

What did he mean? She wasn't sure, but she wasn't prepared to rule anything out. "The bargain's been struck. No changing the terms after the fact. If you wanted restrictions, you should have asked for them up front. Not that I would have allowed for any."

The mer king's hand darted out. He clamped it around her throat. "You filthy creature."

Gertrude scraped at his fingers. She flailed as his huge hand clamped over her gills.

His face gleamed with a strange ecstasy as he pushed her away and above him.

She alternately grasped with her hands and struck out with clenched fists, but the only thing she assaulted was the water frothing between them; his arms were longer than hers. Who did he think he was? You either paid the price or left. Murdering her wasn't an option.

The sea witch wound her tail, preparing to unspool it like a whip. The black snake of her lower body lashed through the water. It lassoed his chest, looping again and again. She squeezed with all her might. She clenched tighter. Tighter. Tighter. His fingers slackened.

She increased the pressure even more. Finally, he let go. Her hands flew to her neck. It felt like he'd cracked it in two, but no, it was still in one piece. She winced as her fingers tapped the tender spots where he'd crushed her gills. "How dare you!" she screamed.

"How dare you demand my descendants!"

The effort of constraining him bled her energy. "It's not like I swam over to your glossy little palace and asked for them. You came to me! And everyone knows when you come here, you pay dear. Did you think I'd make an exception for you because you're so handsome?"

He struggled to free himself from her tail's embrace. "I thought you might be decent about it. I thought the opportunity to save an entire kingdom might fulfill some greater need within you."

Greater need within her? A sour taste filled her mouth. What was he talking about? The back of her neck throbbed. "That sounds like a tricky way to ask for something—a rather big something—and not expect to pay. In case you haven't heard, sea witches aren't in the doing-a-favor business."

She pointed to the swarm of octopuses that had answered the shrill call she'd sent earlier. Gertrude had swam among them since she was a child, and they were friendly to her. Now they gathered on her stoop, tentacles thrusting this way and that. A few were so riled up they were ready to spew venom.

"Pull anything like that again, and they'll spit their ink all over you." Her voice shook from the exertion of restraining him. "Depending on which one gets you first, you'll be dead, maimed, or left scarred and ugly. If they all pile on, you won't make such a beautiful corpse. So if you raise as much as a blasted finger against me one more time, don't think I'll stop them."

"You foul beast," he said.

"Enough with the insults and manipulations." Kings, she didn't like them. "If you want me to save your glittering kingdom, shut your yap and let me do my work."

"Release me at once."

"After you promise to act like every other customer who comes to my lair. In case you haven't noticed, your crown doesn't mean a thing here. The sea witch treats everyone the same."

"How egalitarian of you," he snapped.

She raised her eyebrows. "This isn't personal. It's how we do business. It's how we've always done business."

"That doesn't make it any less offensive."

"Are you done insulting me?" she asked.

He jutted out his chin. His cheek bones were as sharp as rocks.

"Perhaps I need to invite my friends to come closer." She cocked her head in the direction of the octopuses bobbing their heads and rotating their beady eyes at the front of her lair.

The king tried to break free once more, but she held him in place.

"Fine," he said. "I won't assault you."

Very slowly, she uncoiled her tail. She made a wide circle around him as she eased toward the front of her lair. Finally, surrounded by her deadly friends, she felt safe. "I'm going to fulfill my part of our agreement, and I don't want any trouble collecting my payment when I'm done."

He didn't say yes, and he didn't say no.

"Do you understand? If I save your kingdom, you must give me your second son and–"

"The second son of every first son thereafter. I

understand!" Sound waves rocked through the water.

Part II: Second Sons

The first phase of the project took several long and exhausting days. A crew of octopuses dug ditches to carry molten lava across the ocean floor to a moat a second crew of tentacled workers tunneled around the mer kingdom.

The octopuses came to Gertrude's aid because with her hair that was more like an appendage than a mane they believed her to be one of their own.

While they worked, the ocean's temperature continued to drop. When it reached below freezing, blocks of ice formed and drifted to the surface. A few mermaids died, but the king didn't attack Gertrude again. Although whenever she saw him watching from a distance, she touched her neck.

The last day came. She lured five Great Whites with a potent chaw of smashed fish guts and jellyfish larva simmered with a dash of the mermaid's singing voice. The bewitched sharks smashed their snouts like battering rams against the wall of the volcano near its base. Gertrude feared the entire mountainside would crumble; lava would overwhelm the channels, making a burnt, barren wasteland for miles. But when the reverberations stopped, big boulders landed upon other big boulders forming a new wall. The lava seeped from a tall, thin crack. The ditches filled slowly, and the lava flowed toward the mer kingdom. Once the moat filled, it took half a day for the ice to melt and another half a day for the water in the kingdom to rise.

An inner glow warmed Gertrude. She'd never seen Beulah achieve anything as impressive.

When she went to collect her payment, a horde of mermen barred her entrance to the palace with sharp spears. "How dare you?" she screeched, fists balled and flailing. "I upheld my side of the bargain. The king must pay!"

The guards were like statues. They offered no response to her tirade.

Gertrude considered her options. She could cut the supply of heat by sealing the fissure in the volcano wall with an incantation, or maybe draw down a storm that would blast the kingdom to bits.

Two figures swam toward her.

The sea witch's heart leapt. A mermaid led a young merman by the hand. When they were close enough to exchange words, Gertrude noticed the mermaid's crown, and that her eyes, tinged with red, glistened with tears. The queen clung to her second-born son and glared at Gertrude as if she were a demon.

Did the queen not care that her entire kingdom had been saved?

Apparently, not. For she said nothing—nothing!—to acknowledge what the sea witch had done. The queen only held her son close, then watched him swim past the stoic guards with her swollen eyes.

After his mother retreated, the mer prince faced Gertrude. His flinch told her what he thought of her. "What do you want with me?" he sneered.

The sea witch ignored his curled lip. "We're going on a journey. You're going to be my companion."

First, Gertrude led him to her lair. She sorted through her potions and spells. The collection of cloudy jars and bottles clinked against one another as she searched for the one that would transform her servant's tail fin into a pair of human legs. When she finally found the orange-red draught, she looped the vial's bronze chain around her neck.

A monstrous pile of old clothes beckoned. Whenever ships wrecked, and humans died, they drifted to the bottom of the ocean wearing these things. She pushed her way through the stack, grabbing one garment after another.

"What are you doing?" the mer prince asked.

Gertrude held up a ruffled shirt. Once it had been white, but now a stain of smoke and black colored it. "We might need these when we get to land. Humans always wear them."

"Don't expect me to wear that rag," he said.

Gertrude dropped it. She didn't really want to wear any of the clothes either. "I don't know what to pack for the trip." She sagged onto a stack of splintered crates.

"I brought nothing but myself here, I'll take nothing but myself there."

Gertrude gazed around her lair. She'd never lived anywhere else, and now that the day had come when she would finally leave, a sense of despair washed over her.

The mer prince crossed his arms. "Well?"

"I didn't realize how attached I was to my home," she whimpered.

"This hovel?"

"It's a lair, not a hovel."

The mer prince rolled his eyes. "It's full of things no one else wants, garbage and trash. The smell is foul too. You should be glad to leave."

She wanted to scratch out his beautiful aquamarine eyes so he couldn't use them to condemn her anymore. "We're not all born royal," she huffed.

He swam away from her.

She bolted after him. "Where do you think you're going?"

"You want to find land? Follow me."

Gertrude cast one last longing gaze back at the sole, blue-ringed octopus who hovered in the sea weeds. She waved goodbye before she turned to follow her prince.

He swam toward the open sea.

He cut through the water so fast, she feared losing him. "You're bound to me." Gertrude screamed at him. "Do you understand that you'll die if you break the agreement your

47

father made?"

"We're all going to die, anyway."

"Yes, but your death will come much sooner if you defy me."

The young merman looked as if he wanted to throttle her but kept his arms rigid by his side. "Death would be preferable to serving an ugly cow like you." He favored his father through and through.

§ § §

Gertrude dragged her aching body onto an isolated stretch of sand and gulped air. It had been a long and arduous swim with little rest. Her long black tail dangled in the ocean.

The mer prince—his name was Drake—stretched beside her. "Now what?" he panted.

Gertrude took the vial from her neck and handed it to her charge.

"What's this?" he asked.

"Drink up."

"What is it for?"

Gertrude pulled more of her body onto the sand. An enormous octagonal tower shaded the beach. "You need legs."

Dreaming of the Sea

He tried to hand the vial back to her. "I don't want legs."

"We're not returning to the sea."

Drake's face darkened. A thunderstorm gathered in his piercing blue eyes. He tried to shove the small bottle back into her hand again. "I'm a mer prince. I belong to the sea."

Gertrude rolled over and dug her elbows into the wet sand. She crawled farther up the beach. A quarter of her tail remained in the water. She'd never realized it was so long. She felt a sharp prick. Something bounced off her shoulder.

Drake had thrown the vial at her. If he didn't do what she said, he was going to die. If he died, she was going to be left in this strange new world all alone.

She reached for the potion. Once she had the vial in hand, she slammed her elbows into the beach again. Inch-by-inch, she pulled herself from the sea. When every last bit of her was on dry land, she let her upper body drop. The wind filled her lungs and left her drunk with joy. She just needed a minute to gather her strength. Then she would force Drake to drink–

A ripping sensation tore from her waist downward. Gertrude screamed as she doubled over. Heat seared the surface of her body. It felt like she was being skinned alive. An invisible force yanked on the roots of her hair. Gertrude moaned.

The vial slipped from her hands.

§§§

Gertrude's cries gouged Drake's ears. He returned to the sea. Underwater, the spikes of sound became manageable. He considered swimming home to the mer kingdom—until caution took hold. The boundaries of his imprisonment weren't established, and he wasn't sure what would happen if he violated them. Despite his bravado, an instantaneous death held no allure for him.

He swished his tail in frustration. Sacrificing his freedom to save the mer kingdom had sounded more palatable when he was still in the palace, surrounded by shimmering gemstones and shells, servants and young mermaids who gazed at him with longing. Now the brutal truth smothered him. Gertrude was an ugly beast with her black, snake-like hair and greasy, scaly skin. The smell of her made him gag.

Drake thrashed beneath the waves. What would happen when his oldest brother had his second son? Would Drake be released, free to return home?

Not if he drank that potion. He would die on land, a human—and a parasite of the sea. Drake stilled.

The witch had fallen silent. Perhaps the transformation had killed her or someone had murdered her.

He shot to the surface.

A naked human waited there, a female with jet black hair that cascaded to her waist. The long dark waves spread around her shoulders and chest, protecting her modesty to a degree. However, her endless pale white legs that met at the V of a dark triangle were clearly visible. Slim, but shapely, hips curved from her tiny waist.

Curious as to who this creature might be, Drake swam toward the shoreline. When he got closer, he bobbed in the waves, scanning the beach. The sea witch was nowhere in sight. He approached the sand.

The woman met him at the water line and crouched. She handed him the sea witch's vial. "You must drink this."

"Where is the witch?"

The woman's eyes widened. "Do you think you can evade your yoke with silly games?"

"Then you haven't see her?" How long had it been since he'd left Gertrude on the beach?

The sun was setting and a pale moon was visible in the graying blue sky above the woman's head.

"What kind of stupid question is that?" she asked.

Taken aback, Drake studied her emerald eyes. "I led the sea witch here. I left her lying on the sand in agony." The idea to search for tracks came to him. But to see farther, to follow after her, he would need to leave the water. He would have to take the potion.

The female held out the small vial filled with orange-red fluid. "Drink up."

This time, Drake took the small glass container. "Then you saw her? She gave this to you to pass on to me?"

The woman's puzzled expression made him wonder if perhaps she was simple-minded.

Drake chided himself as he untwisted the vial's tarnished silver cap. He shouldn't have stayed underwater so long.

The mer prince swished his shimmering gold tail fin one last time before swallowing the vial's contents in a single gulp. Within seconds, he writhed on the beach. The vial rolled from his palm.

The woman watched him, her dark eyes filled with curiosity.

Drake gritted his teeth. He would not shame himself by screaming out in front of her.

The blade of an invisible knife cut deep into his abdomen. It moved down the length of his tail. He became lightheaded. The world seemed unsteady around him. He forgot about the woman and the sea witch as excruciating pain enveloped his lower body. He pressed his hands against his hips, then raised them to examine his fingers. He expected to find smears of blood, but marveled to find the digits clean. Although he wouldn't have believed it was possible, the pain increased in magnitude. He curled up into a ball and bit his tongue to keep from wailing.

The woman said nothing.

The transformation ended as abruptly as it had begun. Drake unclenched his body. Naked, he now possessed strange genitalia, and two hairy legs extended from there. A strong wind blew in from the sea. The grit of sand prickled against his bare skin.

The woman wasn't far away.

"I have to find the beast who brought me here," he told her.

Confusion bled across her features. "I had no idea the spell would ruin your mind," the woman murmured.

Drake studied her silky complexion, the graceful nose, and pearly teeth. If only he didn't have to search for the witch, he could stay here with her. But he needed to find Gertrude, he needed to know how long his invisible leash was. He tested his legs as the woman watched.

Someone yelled.

Drake turned.

A tall man with a straight back approached. Thick, dark hair reached past his shoulders. His cheekbones were high and flat, he wore a long black coat and baggy garments covered his legs. Despite a long pole he gripped in one giant hand, he walked with a deep, smooth stride. "Hail to both of you."

"Hail," Drake said.

The woman sidled to Drake's side and slid behind him. Drake instinctively dropped his arms and clasped his hands in front of his exposed genitalia.

"You're not from around here." The man kept his distance, but his sonorous voice rang above the crash of the waves.

"We're lost," Drake said. They stood at the head of what appeared to be a long island. Now that he had a better lay of the land, he realized there was only one direction to go. South. Perhaps the man had passed Gertrude.

The man contemplated the pair. "You both need to get dressed. Although the ranchers on Three House Island might appreciate the sight of her, she'll be treated roughly, I assure you. And you—" He held Drake's gaze. "—let's just say it would be dangerous."

"We don't have any clothes," the woman said.

The man speared the beach with his pole made of burnished wood. He handed the woman his black coat. It reached her calves. "Wait for me on the other side of the lighthouse. I'll bring you some blankets and things to wear."

"Have you seen any other strangers on your walk today?" Drake asked.

"No. Have you lost someone?"

The woman pinched Drake's arm. "No," she said.

The tall man doffed his hat and bowed his head in a single motion before marching off in the direction he'd come from.

The woman pulled Drake toward the lighthouse.

He resisted. "I have to find Gertrude!"

The woman pointed to herself. "I'm Gertrude."

Drake laughed as he reached for a curl of her hair and twined it around his fingers. With his other hand, he grazed her shoulder. "Your skin is so soft, your hair so fragrant." He dropped his hands. "Everything about the sea witch is foul."

The woman held up her hands and flipped them front to back. "The devil never told me that when I came on land I

55

would become beautiful."

Gia continued to marvel at herself. She gazed down at her graceful forearms, taut belly, slim hips, long legs, and pebbly toes.

The wonder in her eyes convinced Drake of what her words could not. "It's incomprehensible." He followed her to the far side of the light house.

Gertrude gave him a tentative smile, her pink lips blossoming like some rare flower.

He tried to retain the image of her hideousness, the horrid, bloated face of the witch who'd taken him from his kingdom as ransom. But the more he looked at the woman beside him, the more the memory of who Gertrude had been washed out with the tide.

Drake insisted she change her name.

Gia Chantal was born.

§§§

Gia and Drake arrived in Liberty City following the stock market crash of 1873. Nervous investors who balked at putting money back into an exchange that had ruined them twelve months earlier spoke of little else in the cafes and bars around town. However, Drake was drawn to the waves of power that broke against human dreams and aspirations. His was a compulsion to surf.

To augment his financial instincts, he performed meticulous research for every proposed investment: He analyzed the prospectus, business plan, and press releases. He studied any ongoing publicity regarding the venture. After interviewing the key players, he would cross the channel to Three House Island. The mer prince preferred the isolated island where the wind roared like waves–the leash of the curse extended that far (another fifty miles and the mer prince gasped for air like a fish flopping in the dirt)–to the landlocked city where Gertrude made her home. After a week spent on the beach, he could reliably predict whether the business would succeed or fail. It only worked with public offerings riding the zeitgeist of collective emotion. The limitation was minor. In four years, Drake amassed a comfortable bank account in the name of Gia Ventures. Within a decade, she was independently wealthy. He expanded into international investments, and money ran through their hands like water.

On a particularly steamy afternoon in 1931, Gia conversed with a psychic over an exquisite cappuccino in the village. Curious about many things, the sea witch quizzed the woman about Drake's uncanny knack for investments.

"Where was he born, dear?" the psychic asked.

"His childhood was bound by the ocean...I forget the name of the island."

"Emotions drive financial markets, much like the phases of the moon drive the tide. Being close to the sea in his heart would go a long way to explain his consistent successes."

"Mmm." The answer satisfied Gia. "And what of his Puritan inclinations?"

The psychic raised one shoulder. "His single passion is the markets."

Gia's vision blurred as she surveyed the coffee house's dark-paneled interior. She brushed away hot tears with a napkin crushed in her fist.

Drake served her, but he would never love her. Not even her spells and potions could breach the impregnable fortress that enclosed his heart. Her only solace: she'd learned to fulfill her grasping desires elsewhere.

A young man ordered an espresso at the bar. The urge to drag her fingers through the dark waves of his hair swept her perpetual melancholy out to sea. "Delicious," she murmured.

"You're quite shameless, my dear."

"Indeed." Gia had yet to tire of her ethereal beauty or the opportunities it availed her. Quantity and variety filled the void left by unrequited love. Young, old, male, female, the sea witch had learned what a plaything was. She patted the psychic's hand. "I'll be right back."

Gia leaned against the polished wood espresso counter, adjacent to the young man who seemed to be searching his pocket for change. Perfect. She thrust some bills at the barista and tilted her head in the direction of her intended conquest. It wasn't the first time she'd introduced herself in such a brash manner.

The barista counted out her change.

She slid it back to him.

"You didn't need to do that," the young man argued.

"Of course, I didn't," Gia replied in her huskiest voice. "But I wanted to."

The young man's eyebrows raised.

"Care to join me and my friend?" Gia pointed to the psychic who waved back.

The economy was crashing again, people were out of work, and the sea witch took advantage.

§§§

59

2002 –

Cole taunted his competition with glistening white teeth and dimples. "Who is going to beat me this time? Anyone?"

Eight mermen countered with exuberant mono-syllabic grunts and whistles.

Almost invisible in the shadow of an ocean mountain's rugged crest, Cole's elder brother remained silent.

Several mermaids lounged on the rocky shelf behind the mermen. One held a pink conch shell so large it took both her hands to bring the sea horn to her lips. When the horn's clarion call pierced the roar of the ocean, the contestant's banter halted.

Cole's mind emptied of everything but the pod of dolphins ahead.

Ten undulating forms shot through the water in that direction.

Cole became one with the ocean. His arms flush against his torso, his sleek profile tore through the temperate water as fast as any sailfish. First to join the group of spotted dolphins, Cole slowed imperceptibly, matching his every sway and flicker to the magnificent fish who were equal to a merman in size and weight.

The pod welcomed him with a chatter of whistles and trills as he swam in their midst. When one shot ahead, Cole raced after the fastest dolphin, creating a blinding burst of bubbles in his wake.

The young mer prince surged alongside the spotted dolphin without thought. Relying on acoustical energy rather than sight, his broad shoulders and slim hips rolled and surged in sync with his new mammalian friend. The mer prince made no effort to corral the dolphin, giving the companion fish free rein would make for a more spectacular finale. When the dolphin angled down to the depths of the ocean floor, Cole's heart thrummed. Deeper and deeper the pair dove. The dolphin shot upward, gaining speed, the mer prince at his side. Two torpedoes, they launched toward the sinuous rays of sunlight above.

Breaking the surface, they shot high in the air, an exuberant pair of spinning, twirling, arcing acrobats of the sea.

In the distance, the mermaids lounging on the rocks cheered.

Too late, nine other eruptions exploded around the pair.

Returned to the sunlight-streaked water, Cole and the winning dolphin circled one another, cavorting and frolicking, clicking and touching their noses.

As the school of mermen passed through the golden gates of their kingdom, Cole's elder brother remained conspicuously sullen.

With his preternatural speed, uncanny ability to commune with dolphins, and gregarious nature, Cole was the beloved brother.

That the young prince would never wear the mer king's crown did nothing to appease the firstborn son's black mood, for his future as king was a burden to him.

§§§

"Cole, darling."

His mother's white knuckles caught his attention first, her hands clasped so tight he feared her fingers might break. "Mother?"

"Swim with me beyond the gates." Her request surprised him. He'd never seen his mother, the mer queen, beyond the perimeter of their kingdom.

Silently, he flipped his way beside her. Although not particularly fast, she was agile and elegant as she led him through the roads of the mer kingdom, paved with shells and winking with the occasional spectacular gemstone.

The mer people who watched mother and son pass bowed their heads in deference.

When they were well beyond the gold-filigree gates, his mother altered her direction. She fluttered her hands as her body rose toward the ocean's surface. She led her son to a sandy strip, isolated within a protective barrier of volcanic rock. She rested her elbows in the wet sand and twisted her fingers as she spoke. "There is no easy way to tell you what I must say."

Cole's forehead tensed in a silent question.

"You've heard tales of the sea witch?"

"A hag who abandoned these waters long ago." Cole cracked his tail dismissively.

A drop of water leaked from his mother's eye. "That is true."

Cole's thoughts jumbled. His mother's strange words and demeanor hinted at something disquieting.

"You have an uncle we never speak of." She pulled something from the interstice of her corselet which she enclosed in her fist.

"A brother of father's?"

His mother placed her free hand over his. "Mer people don't

63

dwell on heartache and loss. We're a joyous kingdom."

"Then why tell me of this uncle now?"

"You must know that he serves the sea witch, as did your great-uncle, Drake."

Cole pulled his hand from beneath his mother's and rolled over to sit with his torso erect as he tried to puzzle the point of this announcement. "Will he be coming back? Is that what you want of me? To help prepare his homecoming?" He peered to the side at her.

She closed her eyes. "No, Cole. You'll be joining them soon."

Cole's chest thundered. "What?"

His mother told the story of the sea witch saving the mer kingdom and of the heinous bargain his great-grandfather had struck. "I'm sorry. I should have told you sooner–"

Cole's tail pounded the beach. Dark fury clotted his throat. "No." He met his mother's gaze. "Knowing I was destined to be a slave would only have robbed me of my freedom sooner." No stranger to royal duty, he grasped the debt that must be paid for the good of the kingdom. And yet– "Are you certain the terms will require me to forsake the sea?"

"All these years, the sea witch has never returned to her

lair."

She opened her fist. A gold signet ring rested in her palm. "Take this. Wear it always as a symbol of my love. You must never think that you are forsaken." Tears streamed down her face.

Cole didn't want the ring. He wanted to race dolphins. To celebrate at every mer feast and gala. To be entranced by mer song. To live with honor among his people. He had no curiosity for other creatures or their way of life. "What will happen if I don't go?"

"The witch will return. She has the power to destroy our kingdom. With a storm, or by some other means, I don't know."

"We survive ocean storms aplenty."

"She has the power to draw a cyclone down to the very bottom of the sea. There would be nothing left of our city but ruin and devastation."

Cole slipped the ring on his finger. "What will you tell everyone when I am gone?"

"Some palatable lie. That adventure lured you away."

Wanderlust struck some mer people, but never Cole. "It's ironic," he said. "That curiosity about humans and their life on

65

land plagues my elder brother."

"It's not ironic, it's tragic," his mother said.

Part III: Interlude

2011 –

Everyone was going on the field trip, even the Mother Superior.

Miriam watched the two buses, dull and orange-yellow, wheeze and cough into the courtyard. Her heart pulsed with unrecognizable tension. Akin to fear, but not exactly. She drifted into the line forming to fill the second vehicle. The fifth person, she entered with two giant steps up. Although she didn't meet his gaze, Miriam could feel the bus driver watching the sisters file in.

The seats were padded, but not soft. Strange smells rose from them, as if dead things, molded and decaying stuffed the weary, dark green leather. Miriam advanced past every row, all the way to the back. There, she twisted in the seat to stare out the large, dirt-flecked window. Two sisters sat on either side of her. They chattered like sparrows around her.

In the convent, Miriam's reputation for silence was admired. Muteness afforded her an unexpected freedom which she cherished. No more need to tell lies about who she was, who her mother was, or where she lived. The heavy burden she'd never realized had bowed her shoulders fell away. She dreamt she was a bird, flying weightless through the clouds, or a fish, swimming light and buoyant in deep water.

When the bus lurched forward, the arms of both sisters shot out to keep Miriam from falling, but neither sister told the teenager to turn around, or face the front.

Miriam watched the stone walls enclosing the convent's courtyard disappear as the bus trundled onto the highway. Her mind drifted.

When the door squealed open again, Miriam squinted. The too-bright sun hurt her eyes. Feeling overexposed, she hung back. One of the youngest sisters, only a few years older than

Miriam herself, held out a hand, inviting Miriam to cross the black-top parking lot and join the others on the endless stretch of sand.

Miriam lifted her head. A salty breeze caressed her cheeks as the ocean's relentless roll onto the beach drew her eyes. The rhythm of the white-tossed waves struck her as something eternal. It pulled at something deep within. Her soul?

She followed the sister across the pavement with tentative steps.

There were so many people of all age and size—girls, boys, men, women—many were almost naked, lounging on towels or blankets, running in the surf and building sand castles with bright-colored shovels and buckets, laughing, screaming, burning in the sun.

Miriam was thankful for her dress that hung past her knees as she followed the sister to the water line. When they reached a narrow gap, free of other people, Miriam stopped to concentrate on the ocean's infinite horizon. A desire—or was it a command? (sometimes it was hard to distinguish between the two)—to commune with the eternal tide seized her. She tugged at her scarred brown shoes and pulled off her drooping socks. She spread her toes. The imprints her bare feet left in the sand as she stepped toward the water delighted her.

Several hours later, the Mother Superior called her flock to make the trip home.

Miriam's heart panicked, a bird dreading the return to its cage. She wished to remain on the beach and sleep beneath the stars as the waves sang their endless lullaby.

She crushed the desire.

Safety was paramount.

No more running away.

Part IV: Bargains

2014 –

Gia Chantal threw open the bedroom curtains in the presidential suite. The barefoot socialite crossed the plush carpet to resettle in front of the antique vanity. She closed her eyes and felt for her hand mirror. Gripping its cool handle, she held it in front of her face for the fourth time that morning. When Gia slowly opened her eyes, the shock of what she saw ran through her—a wrinkle on the outer corner of her left eye. She slammed the mirror down, the force of her rage cracking the glass as chunks of the porcelain blue handle skipped across the vanity's gleaming mahogany surface. Gia dropped her head in her hands and wept.

An awful smell assaulted her nostrils. Faint at first, it became more and more difficult to ignore. The stink was worse than the reek of any city dumpster. She raised her head and brushed her hair from her damp cheeks. A black curl of smoke rose from the shattered mirror to dance in the air.

Gia pushed the vanity hard. She hoped to create some distance between the black mist, its stench, and herself. The wood frame rocked and her stool tipped. As she stumbled to her feet, Gia tripped over her silk dressing gown. The malevolent cloud continued to grow. With one hand pressed against her breast, and the other hovering over her eyes, she inched backward.

A dark voice shook the room. "Sea witch, you grow old. And yet, you expend no effort in fulfilling your primary duty."

It was the devil himself. Gia's gaze darted around the luxuriously appointed room. After all these years, how had he found her? "Yes, of course." Her voice quavered.

"Your life force wanes. Provide an heir to the Black Thorn Throne beneath the waves, or suffer the consequences." A coal-colored hand thrust from the menacing cloud, and its fingers curled as if a rubber sphere sat in its palm. "If this requirement isn't satisfied before you die, the contract will be broken." The fingers squeezed air, but Gia felt the tightening grip of bony claws around her heart. "On the day you take your last breath, rather than harvesting your immortal soul and allowing you an eternity of peaceful slumber, I will assure your soul remains intact with all its crimes etched therein. You've been quite ghastly since last we met, thus the torment will be unimaginable, and it will endure through eternity. There will be no escape. Do you understand?"

"Yes," Gia's scratchy voice rasped.

"Even your days are numbered, sea witch," the devil stormed. "Waste no more of my time."

His knobby talons cast her aside. Her arms floundered, reaching for something to break her fall. But she landed hard on her hip before rolling. The back of her head slammed against the carpet. She dug the heels of her palm into her chest, but the staunching pressure did little to relieve the sensation that it had been split in two with an axe.

The black cloud evaporated, and the smell was gone. The devil had exited as quickly as he'd come, but the bruising pain that twisted Gia's chest remained. Would it stay with her until the bond was paid?

She stared at the geometric pattern of brownish glowing spheres above her, the recess lights in the room's high ceiling. The faintest cacophony of horns honked in the city street below.

§§§

Gia dug through her enormous leather satchel for her smart phone. Although she was 160 years old, give or take a year or more, she looked to be a human in her early forties. Her youthful appearance extended to her intellect. She snapped up new technology as soon as at it was released. Something about her watery nature opened her to novelty, or so a psychic had told her ages ago.

Gia traipsed down the hall. She didn't stop until she reached the marble fireplace in the salon. Drake's favorite painting, Rock and Sea, hung above the mantel. Her fingers traced the gilt frame. She still remembered the day he'd purchased it. With bowed head, Gia considered her old friend. An errant tear stung her eye. As she wiped it away, a high tide of memories surged through her.

Her right hand trembled. Whether from emotion, or laudanum withdrawal, she couldn't say. Of late, refilling her prescription for the tincture of opium had become more and more challenging. The hard street drugs that were easier and easier to obtain made for a jagged ride. She longed for the days when any reputable physician would have prescribed laudanum as a sleeping aid without the awkward questions.

Gia stared at the green-blue horizon of the ocean in the painting for some time. When she realized her cheeks were wet, she dragged the sleeve of her silk gown across her cheek. The conditioned air made the damp cloth uncomfortably cold against her skin. Drake and the past were gone. Now Cole, his nephew's nephew, was her bound second son.

"Cole!" she shouted into her voice-activated smart phone. "I need you downtown, immediately. Don't call me back, and do not text. I want you in my suite. We have to talk face-to-face."

She slouched through the penthouse suite, her heart still aching from the devil's grip.

With one hand flat against her chest, and the other pressed against her forehead, she searched for some distraction, some way to kill time until Cole arrived. A social media mastermind, he'd know how to go about finding her an apprentice in this too-modern era that no longer believed in creatures like her.

Perhaps he could create a campaign. She pulled open the living room curtain.

Maybe a billboard in Freedom Square?

§§§

Cole shifted and pumped the Jag's gas pedal. He'd be in Gia's suite in less than an hour. She rarely demanded a face-to-face these days. He liked it that way. It left him free to pursue the activities he enjoyed: researching financial investments, playing with social media, holding court among the most beautiful tourists, and surfing.

Like his uncle Rory, the mer prince who'd served before him, Cole wasn't fond of the sea witch. He kept his distance from Gia. She was getting old, and her lifestyle embarrassed him. She was so obvious, desperate, and indiscriminate when it came to appeasing her sexual appetites.

It had been a long time since she'd called him in to clean up a mess. But there had been a different edge in Gia's voice this morning. There had been none of the sleek purring of the satisfied predator.

A horn blared to the left.

Cole waved his apologies to the cab driver, who flipped him off. Cole shook his head—parasite!

Dreaming of the Sea

He tossed the valet his keys. Everyone at the San Carlos knew Cole and Gia. She'd lived there since the day it had opened in 1904. Everyone who worked there now thought she was the first Gia Chantal's wild, aging granddaughter. They always said, "There's a remarkable resemblance," and, "They could be identical twins."

With a single swoosh, Cole entered the lobby and left the noise of Liberty City behind. He nodded to the concierge. Fresh bouquets of lavender-colored irises flooded the lobby. There were a few hotel guests wandering among the specialty boutiques, but the bank of elevators was empty. Cole inserted his magnetic key and pressed the button for the starred presidential suite.

The elevator opened into the foyer of her rooms.

"Gia," he called.

"Cole!" she rushed toward him, the wide silk sleeves of her dressing gown fluttering. "Darling, thank you, for coming."

Even though her gratitude caught him off guard, he managed to cross his arms and dodge her embrace. She squeezed his shoulder instead. Her well-manicured nails dug into his muscles.

"What's going on?" Whatever it was, she was acting

strange.

She dragged him into the enormous living room. "Coffee? Tea? Lunch, perhaps?"

The San Carlos had the best and most exotic juice bar in the city. "Kale juice," he said.

Gia tsk-tsked. "Always so pure." She buzzed the intercom and placed his order.

"Anything else?" the on-duty butler asked.

"A bottle of Agata Malbec."

Cole didn't comment on Gia's choice. Instead, he surreptitiously searched for her hand mirror. In the mood she was in, he wouldn't be surprised to see a couple lines of coke drawn across its reflective surface. She was still a beauty, but pale purple half-moons hung beneath her eyes, and tiny broken veins blotched what had once been flawless, cream-colored skin. Her lipstick bled into a web of otherwise invisible cracks, and when she forget to pluck them, a wild gray hair would shoot from her eyebrows.

She fidgeted while they waited for room service.

The balmy spring weather, and unremarkable traffic Cole had driven through to get there, challenged their efforts at small talk.

She steered the conversation toward her investments. "How did the meeting with AR Wear go?"

"Interesting," Cole said.

"Always so tight lipped."

"Their Self-Get-Go campaign has raised over $50,000. That's strong public interest."

"Will we make the investment?"

"I'm still pulling everything together for the final decision."

The elevator dinged. The butler entered with an oversized tray. He opened Gia's bottle of wine and poured her a glass. When she was settled, he attended to Cole's juice. He squeezed a lemon then pressed a stub of ginger root. The results dribbled into the dark green liquid.

Cole thanked him.

Gia had not. As soon as the elevator closed on the butler's departure, she leaned forward. Pink rings rimmed her eyes. "I need to find an apprentice."

Cole set down his juice.

"If you help me do this, I'll release all the second sons of the mer kings from my debt."

"I'm listening."

Gia poured herself another glass of wine. "I'm bound to find the apprentice who will replace me when I die."

"Why the sudden urgency?"

"Let's just say, I received a reminder of my obligations this morning."

"What will your replacement do? Move into the presidential suite and pick up where you left off?"

"That would be easy, wouldn't it? No, she'll have to return to my lair with me."

Cole choked on a swig of kale juice. "You'll take her down below?"

"Yes."

"You have the power to transform a human into a sea creature?"

"Yes."

"But not me?"

"No. It was a one-way ticket for you. I'm sorry..."

Cole performed the mental calculation. He'd never be able to return to the sea himself, but no mer king's second son would ever have his tail fins taken from him again. "What's your time frame?"

"As soon as possible. Set all your other work aside."

He leaned forward, elbows resting on his knees. "So how

will this work?"

"When you have the candidate, we'll drive out to Three House Island together. I'll have the potion she needs to drink to transform. I'm amphibious. I'll need nothing other than to soak on the beach for an hour or so. We'll swim to my lair, and you'll be free. No more second sons will be called."

Blood rushed in his ears. Free of Gia? He'd always expected to die, like Drake and Rory, hog-tied to the sea witch with an invisible cord. Now she'd be gone. His mind whirred. Surely, there was some teenaged, misfit, runaway, mental patient who'd find becoming the sea witch's apprentice a step up from their present situation. He just had to locate her.

"I'll create a social media campaign. Something really slick. I've got over twenty million users on Bird, and my Cork board following is climbing every minute." He pushed his fist into his palm. "Maybe augment it with some traditional media, take out a personal ad in every paper in the country."

He was going to be free. He just needed to make sure he chose the right person. Only someone who's circumstances would improve.

"She'll lose her looks," Gia said.

"Right," Cole mused.

Gia's hand waved from her head down to her hips. "I don't look like this beneath the sea."

He'd heard the stories when he was growing up. "Is that why you've never gone back?"

"Just know, the pretty girl you hire won't be as pretty once she swims beneath the sea with me."

Cole didn't think it was a showstopper, but he'd consider it when selecting the final candidate.

"What are you going to do?" she asked.

"I'll approach it like a job interview. Make it sound very intriguing. An opportunity to travel to a new environment—live a life they've never been able to imagine."

"She'll have to stay with me and take care of me until I die." Gia's face twisted into a grimace.

Apparently death frightened her, but Cole didn't probe. He continued building his mental list. "Lots of girls are okay with providing living assistance. Maybe someone with training to be a nurse's aide?"

"I don't think that's necessary." Gia poured herself another glass of wine. "But maybe it's best if she doesn't have family."

"Right, an orphan." He fell back into his thoughts. He needed to get back to his room, turn on his computer, and strategize. "Is that it?"

"Yes."

"I need to develop the campaign details. After I identify a viable pool, maybe twenty to interview, I can whittle it down to five–"

"Two."

"All right. You make the final call."

Gia smiled. "Thank you, Cole."

Cole downed the last of his juice. "Better get going."

"Keep me posted."

When Cole crossed the San Carlos lobby, he was dancing.

§§§

Cole stopped by the French Restaurant for an espresso.

"You're in good spirits," Marco, the bartender who worked every afternoon, commented.

As often as Cole had dreamed of the sea, he'd never believed he might go home until today. And then Gia had smashed his instant of hope, just as he was imagining his return. He set the white china cup down. The strange premonition continued to intrude. He resolved to bury it.

"Did the blue bird of happiness fly away, mi amigo?"

Cole met Marco's gaze. "Gia's getting old, and she needs

me to find someone to help out around the penthouse."

"And that makes you sad?"

Sad? Not exactly.

"She's your great-aunt or something?"

"Something," Cole said.

"What are the hours?" Marco asked.

"Full-time."

"Twenty-four-seven?"

"Pretty much," Cole said.

"That's too bad. I have a niece in night school. She's looking for a job in the mornings."

"She doesn't want this job."

"No? I thought your Gia was wealthy."

"She is, but she's also certain to make your niece miserable."

Marco shrugged. "She's going to be miserable if she doesn't find a job."

Cole patted the man's shoulder. "I'll keep an eye out for something else for her. If I hear of something, I'll let you know."

The man seemed disappointed, but Cole needed to find someone who didn't have an uncle, or mother, or father who would notice when she left and never came back.

Back in his room, Cole loosened his tie and kicked off his loafers. Around the island, when he wasn't in his board shorts, hanging out in the waves, he lived in Bermudas and leather sandals.

He flipped open his laptop and ran some search strings for runaways. The results reminded him he needed to tread softly. Maybe keep things scaled back. Rather than a massive international campaign, something local might be just the thing. Liberty City and the neighboring burroughs had an enormous population of runaways. He just needed one. He buzzed the front desk.

"Yes, Mr. Cole?"

"I need a copy of the *Liberty Voice* delivered to my room for the next five days."

"Would you like that delivery to begin today or tomorrow?"

"You have today's copy?"

"I do, Mr. Cole. I can send it now."

"Along with some salmon tartare?"

"It's on its way."

Cole stretched. If he used the local papers, focused on his

local Bird followers, and maybe posted on the most popular local Cork boards, that would probably be a big enough net.

The presidential suite had a nice office that looked very official. Holding the interviews there would keep things from getting too personal. Maybe he could work out something with the door man, to send them up the service elevator if they looked too raggedy.

§§§

After studying the ads in that day's *Liberty Voice*, Cole went to work on drawing up one for the sea witch's apprentice.

Wanted: *Unattached, 18-21 year old female, seeking full-time employment. Unattached* was more comprehensive than single. He didn't want some single lady with five-hundred friends on Facebook or a large extended family. He needed a loner. The girl could be as young as fourteen or fifteen, but the lines would blur; he'd most likely get a pool of applicants between the ages of 15-24.

Physically demanding (she would be swimming to the sea witch's lair, and someone weak or sickly couldn't make it), *twenty-four-seven, care-taking gig of elderly patient with challenging disposition.* (The poor girl would have to take care of Gia until she died.) *Entry-level position. No degree, training, or prior experience required. Requires travel availability. Will live on site. In addition to salary, a stipend will be provided for meals, clothing, and personal expenses. Sorry, no pets.* (The last thing he needed was some nut job who was more attached to her cat than a mother was to her kid.) *Must love the ocean.* (Because that's where you're going to spend the rest of your life.)

Cole worked on a yellow legal pad. What about an essay? He tapped the eraser against the pad. Best to keep things simple. *Family history. Medical history.* What about a drug history? Did he care whether or not they took drugs? Maybe it would be better to make that assessment in person. *Employment History. Why are you interested in this position?* Share your love of the ocean. Why do you love the ocean? Do you love the ocean, why? *Tell us why you love the ocean.*

Cole re-read the final copy several times. When he had everything the way he wanted it, he switched on his computer. He made a list of all the sites where he wanted to post the ad. He checked the time. Already past midnight. He'd get up early in the morning to surf. Time in the ocean calmed his mind.

Obscure details would float to the surface. He could put any final touches on the ad before submitting it to the online sites. He wanted all the posts up by noon tomorrow.

He briefly considered hiring some temporary workers to handle the load, but he didn't want anyone asking too many questions or volunteering someone they knew for the job. That would get uncomfortable—just like it had with Marco. No, Cole would handle this project and all the details himself.

§ § §

The next morning, Cole rose before the sun. As usual, he beat everyone else to the water. He paddled toward the horizon to position himself for the perfect wave. When it came, he timed the swell and rode it all the way in. Surfing came naturally to him. Although his tail fin was gone, his balance, grace, and sense of oneness with the ocean remained. Maybe after Gia returned to the sea, he'd take off and chase all the big waves around the world.

By the time the next surfer arrived, Cole was ready to get back to work.

He stared at the ad. Cole needed someone who could care less about their physical appearance. Someone who would be unaffected if they became as hideous as the stories said the sea witch had been. How to phrase it? Plain appearance a plus? No, a direct reference to explicit physical characteristics was dicey. Perhaps, modesty a plus. Again. Not the right tone. *Opportunities to socialize will be restricted.* That would keep away the party girls. He inserted *severely* before *restricted*, then: *Please include a recent photo with your application.* He'd cull the pretty ones himself. *Only applicants under serious consideration will be contacted.* Even though the rejection process could be automated, he didn't want to send out thousands of form letters. Eventually, he'd need to erase his digital trail. The smaller and more inconspicuous it was, the easier it would be to eliminate.

He spent the rest of Wednesday morning uploading the ad on various sites and submitting it to the local papers.

§§§

By Thursday morning, there were already 225 applications in the inbox he'd routed to collect all the submissions. He flipped through each one, assessing the attached photos. He deleted the applications for all the girls who looked too attractive— about 40%. Then he put a call into the most unethical shrink he knew, one who would provide what he needed without any pushback.

"I need a psychological profile developed."

"Sure," the shrink said.

"I'd like to forward you some essays. There's going to be quite a few. I need you to handpick the ones that represent the most socially isolated and least self-absorbed. There's going to be a lot. I need you to select the top twenty."

"Anything else?"

"Ability to handle change or a disruption in their routines would also be an asset. In particular, someone who's geographically flexible."

"A globetrotter? Adventure seeker?"

"Thinking more along the lines of someone who's adaptable."

"Compliant?"

Cole stared out his window at the ocean. The weight of the task Gia had assigned him settled in. He didn't want to condemn anyone to the yoke of servitude he lived under, but this was the only chance to free himself and his people. He had to trust that all the measures he was taking would zero in on the one person who could benefit from such an onerous agreement.

"Cole, compliant work for you?"

Or was he fooling himself? Was that an impossibility? "What kind of person would be naturally compliant?" he asked.

"Someone who's conflict averse—someone without a strong direction of their own. A lot of folks are satisfied to follow instructions."

"Fine, include compliant in the assessment."

"When will I be getting these?"

"I'm going to send you the first batch in a minute. A little over a hundred."

"Whoa, that's a lot."

"There's going to be a lot more."

"What's your turnaround?"

"As fast as possible."

"Of course."

"Don't waste your time. I only want the ones who are a perfect fit."

"Will do."

"I'll be sending you batches every day for the next thirteen days."

"I'll get right on it."

"Send the bill to Gia at the San Carlos."

After Cole hung up, he checked his inbox again. A hundred more applicants had come in while he talked to the good doctor. He sifted through the photos and deleted more than half of them. Every now and then, a line of an essay grabbed his attention.

I need this job so bad.

Please, consider me. I've been on the streets since I was ten.

Anything would be better than ho-ing myself out to the filthy johns around here.

I'm a recovering meth addict. An environment where I can't party would be ideal.

This gig sounds great! I don't like to socialize. I hate people!

What's the salary? You should have included the salary in the ad.

I love the ocean, but I can't swim. You didn't say whether or not I need to be able to swim to be considered for the position.

I'm nineteen. You want to hire me.

I'm super healthy. I won't call in sick.

I've never had a job, but I need one RIGHT now.

Every plea hit Cole in the solar plexus. These girls were

desperate, and he was preying on their misery. He pulled out his phone again to call Gia.

"Is something wrong?" she asked.

"Why now?"

"I don't understand what you're asking."

"You've been living on land for over a hundred years. Why do you all of a sudden need an apprentice?"

Dead silence.

Cole watched more applications pour into his inbox. "Gia?"

"He came," she whispered.

"Who came?"

"The devil."

Crap. He couldn't believe this.

"You're not the only one with contractual obligations to fulfill," she said.

"No? Enlighten me."

"Each sea witch makes a deal with the devil himself."

Of course, he should have seen this coming a mile away. "Go on."

"In return for the powers granted us, he demands we take on an apprentice to succeed us—and when we die, he takes our souls."

"Your soul?"

"It's not as bad as it sounds."

"I can't help you do this Gia."

"Why not?"

"I can't be responsible for some desperate human girl losing her soul just because she's lost, or disenfranchised, or damaged."

"If you don't help me, you and your mer princes will be bound to the next sea witch."

Not if Gia died before he did.

"Cole, if I don't find an apprentice, the devil won't take my soul. I'll suffer for eternity for every heinous thing I've ever done. There'll be no reprieve. I won't...that can't happen." Her voice broke.

Cole felt a spasm of sympathy. He'd never encountered this Gia, driven by despair, rather than desire.

"I'm not going to let that happen." Her voice regained its steel.

Cole hardened his own feelings in kind.

"Do you understand, Cole? Either you help me, and free yourself and the rest of your people from the contract your ancestor made with me, or I'll do it myself!"

It wouldn't change a thing for him. He'd never return to the sea. But if he didn't do this, the payment of second sons to the line of sea witches would never end. Cole rubbed his palm from his chin to his forehead. "Do you like being the sea witch?" he asked her.

"When I was young, I was resentful."

That sounded honest.

"It was my mother who gave me to my predecessor. I've never forgiven her for that. At the same time, since I've lived on land, I've enjoyed beauty, wealth, and the power that goes with them. I've relished the freedom to do what I want with no repercussions."

Cole tried to focus on the positives, because if he didn't, he wasn't going to be able to do this. "And your apprentice, she'll have the same opportunity to live on land if she chooses."

"Yes."

"But she'll lose her soul?"

"Unless she wants to keep it. But her soul will suffer for eternity for every spiritual crime she's ever committed. And who among us is truly innocent?"

Cole hung up the phone. If he didn't help Gia, she would find an apprentice some other way. At least this way, he would be free of her demands for the rest of his life, and his people would be free of her and any other sea witch forever.

In the end, Cole was a pragmatist.

Part V: The Sea Witch's Apprentice

Miriam stole around the alcove's railing, quiet as a wisp of mist. She wanted to hear what the two sisters said. The desire puzzled her. Most often, she distracted herself with romantic daydreams and noble fantasies while she worked, preferring to ignore the pious conversations most sisters used to disguise petty gossip. Miriam had few illusions about the urges that lurked beneath solicitous smiles. Beyond the convent's walls, postures of caring and concern were used to gain access to the secrets and horrors most kids hid–information that could be used to further detonate their lives.

But this morning, she was eager to hear what the sisters were saying. One of them was so emphatic, her voice raised to the forbidden level of a yell. The other sister tried to calm her. They paid Miriam little attention as she sorted through the votive candles in the convent's small chapel. It was one of her daily chores. She replaced wax stubs with fresh ones, collected the coin offerings deposited in the two wooden boxes that stood in each corner of the alcove, and dusted the railings and small bits of exposed shelf.

The overwrought sister held a newspaper. "Have you seen this ad?"

The other sister adjusted her glasses and peered at the proffered page. "It's for employment?"

"Not gainful employment."

"There is nothing wrong with working as a caretaker."

"This is a ruse, a thinly veiled proposition for sexual exploitation."

The other sister studied the page again. "I admit, it is troublesome."

"We must take it to the committee."

"Sister, I appreciate your passion, but adults are beyond our purview. We've discussed this."

The other nun snorted. "Eighteen to 21 is hardly adult."

"Our resources are limited. We can't save everyone in Liberty City. We agreed to focus on the children."

"We're called to be soldiers in God's army. The war won't be won with complacency."

"Nor through prayer?"

"We can't just close our eyes to this kind of exploitation!"

"You must pray upon this, Sister. Pray, pray, pray. You must never underestimate the power of prayer."

The two wandered toward the long hall of administrative offices.

Miriam shadowed the sisters at a distance.

They entered an office briefly, then exited.

Miriam snuck into the unlocked room. The paper perched on the corner of a desk. She grabbed it and fled.

Miriam gasped for breath beneath the mighty oak that guarded the kitchen door. She gazed around the courtyard to insure she was alone before stuffing the paper behind her back, into the tie that served as a belt for her loose dress. Satisfied that no prying eyes spied upon her, she slipped off her simple shoes, reached up to the thick branch overhead, and pressed the soles of her feet against the tree's trunk for leverage. Moving quickly, she climbed as high as she could. Confident no one could spot her, she pulled the paper from behind her back.

A black felt pen had been used to circle the ad. It called for the care-taking of an elderly woman.

Miriam read and re-read the ad. Her careful evaluation produced no sense that sexual exploitation would be involved. In that regard, Miriam trusted her instincts.

§§§

Eighteen-year-old Miriam had recently embarked upon the process of discernment. What would God call her to do with her life? It seemed her overarching need for security had been assuaged, and now other desires rose in her breast.

Miriam studied the ad again.

Sister had been right about one thing. Employment that required no degree or training was suspect. Yet care-taking a bitter old woman sounded like an interesting opportunity.

A sacrificial wellspring surged within Miriam. A font of inspiration, it fed her dreams of drowning herself in some noble cause. Perhaps this could be the first in a long line of

100

many such opportunities. Easing an old woman's suffering. Would that be satisfying?

Miriam contemplated how her life might change if she were to take on such a challenge. Her ignorance of the world beyond the convent walls dead-ended her imaginings. She needed more facts. She studied the ad once more.

Tell us why you love the ocean.

Miriam's hand rested on her breast.

There were two computers in the library. Today was Wednesday. She had five days to draft the essay in her room.

§§§

That night, Miriam began preparing her application. She verified that she was an unattached, eighteen-year-old female, available for full-time employment. She painstakingly transcribed the facts of her family history without emotional embellishment. She assured her potential employer that she was strong and patient. She wasn't patient. How would she tolerate verbal and emotional abuse? That's what a challenging disposition meant, didn't it? ~~I would welcome the opportunity to grow a thicker skin.~~ *I'm quite adaptable to different personality types. I've had to learn to get along with all types* of people, including difficult ones.

True enough.

Due to my circumstances ~~I can't afford~~, I've never had the opportunity to ~~go to college~~ obtain a college degree. Nor have I had the opportunity to seek employment beyond the Sisters of Charity and Grace. However, after embarking upon a period of discernment, I ~~don't~~ can't see ~~my~~ a future with the sisters. ~~I am desperate. I need this job.~~ I know I am ~~the right~~ possibly the best applicant for this position.

Medical History. Excellent. I never get sick and have no chronic diseases. My eyesight is perfect.

Employment. I've worked for my room and board since the day I was born.

Why are you interested in this position? The Sisters of Charity and Grace took me in when I was fifteen years old. While my time here has been productive, I don't see my future as a nun or a sister. I would appreciate the opportunity to embark on a new path. I have no pets. I do not care to socialize.

My single visit to the ocean was momentous. I long to return.

Miriam considered her initial efforts. Tomorrow night she

would try again.

§§§

Every night, for the next five nights, Miriam pulled out her pad of paper and re-read what she'd written the night before. On Tuesday, she folded the polished essay four times and stuffed the square into her bra.

She was relieved to find only two sisters in the library when she arrived, the sister on-duty, Sister Betty, and Sister Nan. Sister Nan avoided computers like the plague, and Sister Betty seemed absorbed with her tasks at the front desk. Miriam dropped off the two books she'd checked out last week—two paperback romance novels. Sister Betty's eyebrows rose with the usual disdain. The sisters frowned upon fiction. They also prohibited waste. When worldly donors bequeathed boxes of chick lit, fantasy, and romance novels, it always provoked a spiritual dilemma, which the sisters resolved by burying the dog-eared paperbacks on the library's back shelves.

See no evil.

Ever since Miriam had discovered them, she'd made a weekly trip to select her allotted two books every Tuesday.

However, that night, instead of heading back to replenish her supply, Miriam headed toward the library's two computers.

She made a point not to look around as she tapped the space bar and waited for the login screen. When it came up, she typed in the generic login and password. Before she pulled the paper from her blouse, she located Sister Betty and Sister Nan. Neither of the sisters had moved. Miriam unfolded her piece of paper and flattened it on the desk. She typed in "job application + unattached female + caretaker." She clicked on the top link. It took her straight to an entry portal. She transcribed the essay she'd labored over for the entire week. After she finished, she clicked open another window to. A search for "image + nun" didn't bring up a picture she could use. She tried "image + plain girl." She settled on a photo of a young woman with similar hair and eye coloring to hers, brown and brown. She did a quick copy and paste.

Sister Betty, quiet for so long, shuffled some papers. Then the nun began to pile books onto a re-shelving cart, each one landing with an audible thud.

Miriam's shoulders tightened. She surveyed her application one more time before pressing send.

Now, Sister Betty headed in her direction.

Miriam tried to focus as she fumbled with the computer keys. She typed in "discernment" and clicked on the first link.

Sister Betty peered over her shoulder. "Finding everything all right?"

"Yes."

"Discernment, that's a great topic to study."

Miriam nodded as she spread her hand and forearm across her essay.

Sister patted her on the shoulder and drifted off.

Miriam exhaled a quiet breath and folded the sheet of paper. This time, she poked it up the sleeve of her sweater. So as not to call undue suspicion to her activities, she headed to the back of the library to get her customary two novels.

Exhilaration coursed through Miriam's veins as she walked back to her room.

§§§

The next day, Miriam itched to return to the library. Had her application received a response yet? As she checked off her daily chores, she tried to come up with a viable excuse for more frequent trips to the library—and more time spent on the computer—since internet use was discouraged.

Nothing came to mind. For the first time since she'd come to the convent, she resented the rules she'd agreed to live by. How did cutting yourself off from the rest of the world make you more pure? Didn't it just make you weak? Yesterday, the collectively and self-imposed boundaries had felt safe. Now, they seemed like some sort of moral deficiency—a lack of clarity and commitment...something suspect. Relying on external restrictions to curtail desires that rumbled in your heart with steady insistence seemed like the coward's way out.

That night Miriam tossed and turned, making argument after argument for greater moral freedom, and wondering what had become of her application. The next day, she prayed for help.

Please, help me come up with an excuse to return to the library and use the internet.

If this was her calling, she believed God would respond. Later that morning, the Mother Superior called Miriam to her chambers.

Miriam's stomach pitched between excitement and dread. Had she been found out?

"Sister Betty tells me she saw you in the library Tuesday night, researching discernment."

"Yes, Mother."

Mother's tight wimple pulled the sides of her eyes up,

erasing half her wrinkles. Two hairs sprouted from a mole on her left check. She wasn't an ugly woman, but none of the sisters wore make up, and as they aged, there was nothing to conceal the toll taken by time.

"We discourage internet use."

Miriam's heart plummeted. How was she going to find out what had happened with her application if she was banned from the library computer? "Yes, Mother."

"Most of the sisters are computer averse. However, at times it can be a useful tool."

Miriam held her body stiff and face impassive.

"I've just had a long chat with Abbot Erickson."

He was the abbot of the Brothers of Charity and Grace.

"He's developed a website, nothing fancy, as an outreach for the population we're targeting with the joint HCST committee."

Healing Childhood Sexual Trauma. Miriam couldn't breathe.

"We need to check the site daily for incoming messages. It would be heartbreaking if anyone reached out to us, and we missed their call."

Miriam risked the slightest nod.

"Perhaps you could add this task to your daily routines?"

"Of course, whatever I can do to help."

Mother pulled a sticky note from the chartreuse pad of post-it notes on her desk, the only splash of color in the entire office. "Here is the web address and login information. We're offering a twenty-four hour response, so choose a time and be consistent."

Miriam picked up the bright green square.

"Print whatever is in the inbox and deliver it immediately to Sister Clare." Sister Clare was the head of the HCST committee. "Don't delay. She'll need to act on the communications immediately. Do you think you can handle that?"

"Yes."

"Thank you, Miriam. That would be most helpful."

"When would you like me to begin?"

"Within the next twenty-four hours."

Miriam floated from the mother's office.

§§§

It took three days before she got her response.

Please call to schedule an interview.

She'd received a password when she'd submitted her application. She used the same password to access the call number.

Although no one in the convent was allowed to have a cell phone, telephone calls weren't controlled as tightly as the internet. There were pay phones in the lobby.

A young man answered the phone. "Cole, here."

Miriam's voice shook.

She had three days to figure out how to cross the bridge to Liberty City for her appointment.

§§§

Miriam gazed around the library as she waited for the two comments from the committee website to print. Every day, there seemed to be at least one or two new posts; all of them accused priests of sexual abuse and molestation. Miriam didn't pay attention to a lot of things that happened around the convent, but she did know that stirring up the priest sexual abuse scandal hadn't been the program's intention. Frankly, she was surprised they hadn't already pulled the plug on the website, or shut down the comments section. Anyone could get online and read them.

When Miriam delivered the pages to Sister Clare, the nun

never asked questions; she just accompanied her strained, "thank you," with a sour smile. Miriam sensed the frustration simmering beneath the mask. They'd intended to hunt the devil beyond the church walls, not the one that roamed within.

The sisters had no idea what life on the street was like for a kid. There were times you got so cold and so hungry–and God never showed up with a warm meal or extra blanket. The only people who did were the ones who wanted something in return. The decent ones asked for some honest labor to be performed: shovel some snow, wash some dishes, stuff like that. But they were as few and far between as the good samaritans, the ones who did it out of some unconfessed need of their own. Most of the kids knew it was guilt. Guilt for having too much now, or guilt for having done–or not done–something in the past. Most of the do-gooders expected you to be grateful. If it had been an okay week, you tried to give them the show they wanted, but if the week had been a bad one, maybe you just grabbed and snarled.

Watching the outrage break through their beatific poses always made for a few laughs.

Miriam blinked. She stood in the church nave. She'd walked from Sister Clare's office in a daze. She couldn't remember the last time she'd thought about her days on the street. For so long now, she'd drifted through life dreaming of some noble future. Although she could never accept the religious stories the sisters taught as fact, Miriam cherished the psychological truths they embodied. She especially appreciated the story about the impoverished stonecutter who'd offered himself, willingly, to a brutal death impaled upon a spike. She gazed at her own palm. Ran her finger along the crease that ran its length. She craved to give her soul to some selfless cause. A passion.

She dropped before the altar of burning candles and prayed.

The idea of stealing money from the collection box for her bus fare came to her.

§§§

Mother Superior sent for Miriam after evening prayers.

Abbot Erickson had in his custody a young female runaway. She'd been abused on the streets. The abbot wished the girl to spend some time with the Sisters of Charity and Grace.

Mother asked Miriam, "Would you be comfortable taking the bus uptown to the abbey tomorrow and escorting her back to us?"

"Yes."

111

"You've become quite an asset to our community," Mother said. "It must be difficult, being the youngest one here and having no peers to share your growing pains with. All young women have them."

"I like the peace and quiet here."

"I understand you read a lot."

Miriam stretched her fingers around her kneecaps through the thin cloth of her dress.

"Most women your age harbor romantic fantasies. They're quite normal. You never interact with men. Perhaps those romance novels you read are an outlet for your urges."

Miriam didn't want to have this conversation with Mother.

"Miriam, there's nothing to be ashamed of."

Miriam stared at the dark whorls on the side of Mother's desk.

The nun shuffled some papers. "You've entered your period of discernment."

"Yes, Mother."

"And you're praying for guidance?"

"Every single day."

"Such enthusiasm is commendable. Perhaps," Mother continued, "being a mentor for others might suit your nature and talents. Have you discerned whether you would be more suited to a contemplative or active service to God?"

"Active."

"Then, this will be an opportunity to test the intimations of the inner calling you hear."

"I'm most anxious to discern my place in the world, Mother."

"Wonderful. Sister Beatrice will accompany you."

"Oh, no, Mother, that's not necessary."

"I beg your pardon."

"I simply meant the sisters appreciate their routines. I could go alone."

Mother shifted in her seat. "Do you perhaps dislike Sister Beatrice? I know she's rather stern. Does she make you uncomfortable?"

Miriam cast about for some plausible excuse for going alone. "Well, I wasn't thinking of myself." Oh, that was good. "I was thinking of the girl." Yes, her story was coming together. She stared out the window at the ancient oak tree. "Perhaps—" She broke her statement on purpose, hoping it made her sound less calculating. "Perhaps I could share some of my past with her. It might make her feel more...accepted."

Mother rubbed her lips.

"It's a silly notion," Miriam said.

"No, your consideration of her situation is commendable. I shall pray upon it."

The flying bird of Miriam's heart crashed into the paned window of Mother Superior's caution.

"Of course, Mother."

"Wouldn't you be afraid? Traveling in the city alone? After all these years, you might have troubling memories. You suffered so much there."

"I wouldn't be alone, Mother. My Heavenly Protector is always with me."

Mother's eyes widened, a real smile touched the edges of her mouth. "Your spiritual growth has surpassed all hopes I might have harbored on your behalf."

Miriam bowed her head. She hoped it made her appear humble.

§§§

An hour later, Miriam pushed her curtains open. The moonlight cast strange shapes around her small room. She returned to her bed to stare at the ceiling. If God existed, she had no doubt He wished her to be in Liberty City tomorrow afternoon.

Indeed, her prayers of discernment had been answered. She would find her place in the world—the duty she'd been born to shoulder. She pressed her hands flat on the mattress beside her. If she didn't, she might leap from her bed and prance.

The money she'd stolen for her bus fare hid in the toe of a grayed sock at the bottom of her pasteboard chest of drawers. She wouldn't need it now. On Thursday, Miriam would add it to the deposit of whatever she took from the collection boxes that day. She released a long exhale. Stealing always left such a bitter aftertaste.

Miriam slid from her bed and prayed a most fervent prayer for Sister Beatrice. "Please, dearest Father in Heaven, if this is my true path, strike her ill. Let it be serious enough that she can't step one foot beyond the convent walls tomorrow, but not deathly."

§§§

Mother gave Miriam two bus passes, one for her and one for her charge. Next, Mother handed Miriam a flip phone. The young woman balanced it, with the two passes, on her knees. She clutched the sides of her chair to contain her elation.

Sister Beatrice was en route to the hospital. Appendicitis.

115

"You're sure that you're comfortable going alone to pick up the girl?" Mother asked.

"Will Sister Beatrice be all right?" Miriam asked.

"She'll be fine. It was just so unexpected."

Miriam bit her lower lip as she risked picking up the cell phone. She didn't need her joy spilling out, blaring some supernatural alert to Mother. "If I have any problems, at all, I'll call you."

"If it's severe, dial 9-1-1 first."

"Yes, of course, Mother. Thank you for reminding me."

Mother glanced at the clock on the wall. "You must leave now to catch the Number 259."

Although her legs were like noodles, Miriam stood up.

Mother came around her desk and squeezed Miriam tight.

§ § §

It was another bit of blessed fortune that the San Carlos was on the same bus route as the Brothers of Charity and Grace.

Miriam looked up at the tall hotel. Cole had told her to ask for the door man, who would direct her to the interview.

A bell dinged. The elevator's gold paneled door slid open. The smell of coffee, flowers, perfume, and rich food assaulted Miriam's nostrils.

A young man, the handsomest she'd ever seen, walked toward her. "Miriam?" The question resonated with dismay.

"Cole?"

"You don't look anything like your picture."

Miriam had forgotten about the fake photo. "Well...that..."

He crossed his arms. "We needed those photos for the evaluation process. I can't allow you to proceed with the interview."

"But I've come all this way—"

"I wish you'd sent a real picture," he said. "It would have saved you a trip."

Visions of herself, old and bored, tottering around the convent, flashed through Miriam's mind. "Please, give me a chance."

"You're not a viable candidate," he said.

"I need this job."

Cole ran his fingers through his thick gold hair. "You don't want it."

Miriam had already decided she wasn't leaving until he offered her the job. "Could I at least bother you for a glass of water?"

"Sure." He turned on his heels.

She raced down the hall after him. They entered an enormous office, three times the size of Mother Superior's. He stalked over to a counter covered with cut crystal bottles filled with different colored liquids. The hard stuff. A clear carafe, coated with the fog of chilled moisture, stood among them. He poured a glass and handed it to her.

She took small sips. Even though he was angry with her, she felt safe in his presence. There were few men, standing this close, who didn't make her cringe or flinch. And even though he'd commented on her appearance, his gaze didn't grope her. "How long have you worked here?"

As if to underscore his resistance to her, Cole crossed his arms. "Twelve years."

"If I'm not right for the position in the ad, maybe there's another opening?"

"No." He held out his hand for the empty glass.

Miriam tightened her grip on the cup. "I came here for an interview. You can't just turn me away because of my appearance."

He half-sat on the edge of the enormous desk. "Gia is difficult. It's complicated."

"I have time." Miriam moved to sit in one of the overstuffed chairs. "Explain it to me."

"We need someone who won't get distracted."

"I'm very focused."

He rubbed his left eye.

"I need a job."

"A girl like you shouldn't have a hard time finding another one."

"A girl like me?" Her breathing came faster. She risked a glance in Cole's direction. He wasn't even bothering to look at her. He was staring out the window, ignoring her question. "What kind of girl do you think I am?"

"You're very attractive."

Her appearance shouldn't have anything to do with her ability to take care of an old lady, but he seemed so dead set on making an issue of it. "I love the ocean. I want to spend more time there."

A storm gathered on Cole's brow.

"That's a plus," a woman's voice said. She swept into the office, wearing only a silken house robe. Her alabaster skin and raven hair made Miriam think of some mythical creature. Her green eyes pierced Miriam's as she settled in the chair next to her.

Miriam took the initiative and held out her hand.

"I'm Gia Chantal." The woman took hold of Miriam's hand and pulled it into her lap.

Miriam swayed forward, following her hand.

"Don't let Cole worry you. I have the final say in the matter. What is your name?"

"Miriam."

"Tell me something about yourself, Miriam. Any reason why I should trust you to care for me in my dotage?"

The woman hardly looked a day over forty. Miriam wondered why she needed a caretaker. "I live in a convent."

"Oh, my goodness! Are you a nun?"

"Oh, no, I've only just entered discernment."

Gia asked her what that meant.

"It's a period where we seek our life's purpose through contemplation and prayer. I've been contemplating and praying over this position, ever since I found out about it."

"Being a caretaker appeals to you, dear?" Gia asked.

"I feel–" Miriam stopped herself. She sat straighter in the chair and pushed her hair behind her shoulders. "I believe there isn't a better candidate."

"Your determination is compelling."

"Thank you."

"I'd like to offer you the job," Gia said.

Miriam burst into a smile.

"No!" Cole shouted.

Gia's right eyebrow raised. "Cole, darling. Did you hope to steal her away for yourself?"

Three shades of red flushed his chin to his forehead.

Miriam's face heated as well.

"When can you begin?" Gia asked.

"The sisters...I must complete a task the Mother Superior assigned me."

"How long will that take?"

"I'll be finished tonight. I can leave the convent in the morning."

"That sounds perfect," Gia said.

"Gia, please." Cole's anger flowed into sadness.

"He can be such a spoil sport," Gia said. "He and all his kin. Where is this convent of yours?"

Miriam gave her the address. She purposefully glued her gaze on Gia's face. Cole's response puzzled her, and she wanted to avoid it.

"I'll send my driver around in the morning to collect you and your things," Gia said. "I'm assuming you don't have much, if you're living with the sisters."

"Your assumption is correct."

"Well, then." Gia stood up. "I'll leave you two to complete the paperwork."

Miriam jumped up to grasp Gia's hand. "Thank you, so much, Ms. Chantal. You won't ever regret giving me this opportunity."

Gia pushed a stray curl from Miriam's face. "I think you're right. I don't believe I will."

§ § §

Cole sat on the other side of the desk. He pushed a stack of papers toward her but said nothing. They looked like standard employment forms. He didn't offer her a pen. Miriam took one from the holder on the desk between them.

"You're making a big mistake," he said.

"That's easy for you to say."

"Actually, it's not."

"Do you think you're protecting me?"

"That's exactly what I'm trying to do." He leaned forward. "But you won't let me."

"Maybe I don't need your protection."

"Maybe you do, and you just don't realize it yet."

"Why do you care?"

"Gia is a witch. You don't want to work for her."

"No, you don't want me to work for her."

Cole came from around the desk and knelt before her.

Miriam felt her eyes widen as she pushed herself as deep into the chair as she could go. What was he going to do? The entire time she'd been with him, she'd sensed no threatening sexual undertones. Had she been wrong?

"Miriam, please," he said. "Walk out of here and never look back."

Her body relaxed. She spied a clock on the mantel. If she was going to pick up the girl at the abbey on time, she needed to leave soon. "Thank you for your interest in my welfare, but I assure you, I know what I'm doing."

"You have no idea," he said.

She spread the papers across her knees. His concern for her pulled an unfamiliar response from within her, a desire to lower her walls. "Fine, tell me whatever it is you want to tell me to convince me this is a bad idea."

His eyes were so bright. He raised his hand as if he was going to touch her, but ran it through his thick hair instead.

"It's not my place to explain."

He didn't want her to take the job, but it wasn't his place to explain—why all the mystery? "Are you afraid of her?"

His face became a screen of turbulent emotions. "I see a light all around you. Please, don't do this."

His sincerity gave her pause. But there was no way she could walk away now.

After less than an hour with him and Gia in the presidential suite of the San Carlos, Miriam's spirit hungered for things she'd never known she'd craved. The convent was so dark, with all its old wood paneling and small windows. Everyone was so dowdy in their dull habits and plain dresses. Riding the bus out of the burrough, and then the subway into downtown, Miriam had been quickly reminded—there were other ways to live.

She didn't want to live on the streets, but she didn't want to spend the rest of her days locked away with the sisters, either. If she saved the salary Gia paid her, who knows how much she might squirrel away before the woman died? Miriam could start a new life then. Whatever sacrifices would be required in the meantime, she'd be glad to make them. It couldn't be worse than sneaking around the convent, reading romance novels, and waiting for her life to begin. And yet, something about Cole's pleading was making her question herself, and recognize her own desperation to sign on the dotted line.

What would she do if he talked her out of it? If she left, right now, without completing the forms?

She couldn't let this hope spill from her hand.

Miriam locked her heart. If she didn't take this job, the road to her future looked long, dull, and dreary, with no exit ramp in view. "She needs someone to take care of her, right? What's wrong with a job like that?"

"One day you're going to understand why I tried to talk you out of doing this," Cole said.

"One day you're going to understand why it's important to follow your heart," she replied. "Even when it looks like it's leading you in the wrong direction."

§§§

The next morning, the Mother Superior sent for Miriam. When she entered the mother's office, Miriam's entire body tensed. Gia Chantal, wearing spiked heels, a gemstone colored-dress, the hemline just above her knees, and a broad-brimmed hat, sat in front of Mother's desk. The nun's face was a stone.

125

"Miriam, please, let me introduce you to Ms. Chantal."

Miriam nodded.

Mother picked up a long paper rectangle. "She's just made a very generous donation to the convent. Please, sit, Miriam."

Miriam perched on the edge of the empty chair next to her new employer.

"Ms. Chantal has come to me this morning with an unusual request."

Miriam decided it would be best to remain silent.

"She'd like to hire an assistant, someone to help her with daily tasks. Running errands, organizing her calendar, handling personal correspondence and such. She's requested you, specifically, Miriam."

Miriam gave her head the slightest bob.

"She'd like you to start today."

Miriam coughed into her hand. "Today, Mother?"

"Her terms of employment are quite generous. There will be a stipend and an allowance for food and clothing."

Miriam goggled at the amounts.

"Do you have anything to say, Miriam?" Mother asked.

Miriam stared at the floor. "I'd like to accept her offer."

"The Sisters of Charity and Grace will bear the loss,"

Mother said.

"Hopefully, the donation will fill the void," Gia quipped.

§§§

Miriam wished she felt more guilt...more regret...more something as she hugged each sister goodbye. She'd lived there for almost a decade and hadn't formed a single close bond. When she reached the younger girl that she'd escorted across town yesterday, it was just another empty hug. For all the show she'd put on for Mother the preceding morning, Miriam had made little effort to befriend the girl or draw her out as they'd ridden across town on the bus yesterday evening. The spiritual high from her successful interview had lingered, and Miriam had resisted coming down to tend her charge. Not that the girl had made any effort to open up, either. And yet, there was a way they understood each other. A bond without words. That's what growing up on the streets gave you: An understanding of survival that went so deep, you'd never begrudge anyone the chance to move on and better their lives.

Miriam suspected she and the new girl were in many ways the same. Last night the girl had slept in the infirmary. Tonight, she'd move into Miriam's room. Tomorrow she'd be dusting the altar and the votive candles. That's how life was on

127

the streets. The revolving doors existed, they were just invisible and didn't make any sound when you passed through them.

§§§

The trip to the San Carlos took less time in a chauffeured limousine than it did by bus and train.

"We'll be in the city for a few more weeks." Gia showed Miriam to an unused bedroom. "Until then, make yourself at home."

When Miriam turned to ask her new employer where they would be going when they left the city, the hall was empty. Where had Gia gone? Miriam stared at all the closed doors. She didn't dare knock on any of them.

§§§

For the first week, Miriam wondered at Cole's warnings. Gia laughed and flirted with Miriam and everyone else. The unlikely pair went out for coffee and tea; there were shopping sprees and expensive lunches—one night, they even went for dinner and a show in the theater district.

The second week, Gia started throwing things. When she screamed for more laudanum, it took her five days to wear Miriam down. The young woman made the long trip to the rundown clinic for the prescription no respectable doctor would fill. It sickened her to watch Gia count the drops into her wine, but at least she slept through the night.

When Cole came by, Miriam was ready to listen to him. He wanted to take her out to lunch, but Gia raged, so they ate an awkward meal in the suite's cavernous dining room. The ceiling was so high, the room itself so big—too big for three people—every word they spoke seemed to echo.

"Gia, do you have family?" Miriam asked.

"If you count the devil as my father."

She wondered if Gia had ever been homeless. Her erratic moods and bouts of self-pity reminded Miriam of the bag ladies she'd encountered when she'd lived on the streets. Abandoned by their parents, their spouses, and/or their children, they were hard to be around. Miriam had made it a point to avoid them whenever possible. But she wouldn't be able to avoid Gia.

"What about your father, Cole?" Miriam asked.

He shook his head.

Gia swooped up the bottle of wine and her glass. "I'm going to take a siesta now. Miriam, be available when I wake up."

"Yes, ma'am."

Miriam and Cole sat silent together for a few minutes. She wanted to ask him so many questions, but he'd warned her she was getting into a difficult situation.

"How are you?" he asked.

"The first week was wonderful."

"And now?"

"She's moody. She's been throwing things."

"It's going to get worse," he said, "much worse."

There wasn't much Miriam could do about it now, other than endure. "Do you know where we're going when we leave the San Carlos?"

"Gia hasn't told you?"

"No."

Cole set his napkin on the table. "Wait here, let me check on her." When he came back, he seemed more relaxed. "She's passed out. We have a few hours. Let's walk over to the park."

Miriam followed Cole out of the suite and across the hotel lobby, into the afternoon sun. The streets were crowded with cars, vans, taxis, messenger bikes, and pedestrians. When they reached the park, they walked for about half-a-mile more. Cole settled onto a bench. She sat beside him. Only inches away. Again, she absorbed how much she enjoyed his physical presence. It was pleasant, but unsettling.

"I can't believe she hasn't told you anything," he said.

"Can you tell me?"

He hunched over his knees, his forearms on his thighs. She resisted the strange urge to rub his bowed back. "You won't believe me," he said. "Maybe that's why she hasn't said anything. Maybe she knows it's so crazy, you won't believe it until you experience it for yourself."

For the first time, Cole's words alarmed her. Or was it the dread rolling from him in continuous waves? Maybe she shouldn't have sat so close to him. It felt like she'd swallowed a piece of scratchy paper that had gotten wedged in her throat. "What are you both hiding from me?" It didn't even sound like she was the one speaking, her voice was so rough.

"I'm a merman," Cole said.

A clipped laugh escaped her lips. She'd never realized he was an actor. He and Gia had never mentioned it. "In one of the shows in the theater district?"

"No, in real life."

Although the playful turn of the conversation didn't match the turmoil she sensed roiling within him, it helped her calm down. "That's an amusing claim, but you have no tail." Miriam

131

was glad to notice her voice had returned to normal.

"She took it."

"Gia took your tail?" Where was he going with this?

"She put a curse on my family. Every second son must serve her."

Miriam blinked in the sunlight. "I'm not following you."

"No, I imagine you're not," he said.

Sometimes delusional people could be brought back to reality if you helped them focus on the simplest elements of their claim. And she had to admit: Cole's claim was becoming as strange as any street person's she'd ever encountered. "Are you a second son?"

"Yes."

Miriam crossed her arms. "What does any of this have to do with me?"

"You're her apprentice."

"I'm her caretaker. The employment form was very clear about my duties."

"You don't get it."

"No, I don't think I do."

"You will, when she takes you down to her lair at the bottom of the sea."

Miriam laughed out loud. Now, she understood his purpose. "You're trying to humor me. You know she's hard to handle and that her moods have been foul this week. You're trying to make me laugh. That's very kind of you. I appreciate it. You're quite inventive."

"I wish that's all it was," he said. "When she ordered me to find her an apprentice, well, that's why I wanted a photo and life history. I wanted to be sure that it would be an improvement for whoever took the job. But this isn't an improvement for you. It's going to destroy you. You're going to be bound to her until she dies, and when she takes you beneath the sea, your whole appearance is going to change. I hate to say it, but you're going to transform into something nasty and repulsive. And that's not the worst of it."

Miriam didn't quite know how to handle his continuing on as if every word he said were true. Should she humor him or make him stop?

"As her apprentice, your soul now belongs to the devil," Cole said.

A bolt of outrage flushed through Miriam. She stood up. "Now, I see you're making fun of me. I had no choice but to live with the sisters for the past decade. I have no family. I have nothing. They took me in, fed me, clothed me, and kept me safe. I was productive, if lonely, during my time with them. There's no reason for you to make fun of my past situation."

He grabbed her arm. "I'm not making fun of you. I warned you not to take this position because I knew the sea witch trafficked with the devil. I should have done more to stop you. Now, it's too late."

What if he was telling her the truth? Miriam sat down beside him again. Impossible. "Have you suffered from delusions for a long time?"

He gripped her arms. "I'm sorry. I was tasked with finding her apprentice. I did everything I could to ensure that someone like you wouldn't be the one. I failed. I'll be set free from my curse, as will all the second sons that come after me. But your enslavement will just be beginning."

"You seem so normal," she whispered.

"Without my fins and gills, I'm as much a human as you."

An unwanted fragment of clarity splintered through her mind. "Is that why the application had the question about the ocean?"

"Yes, because that's where you're going to live for the rest of your life."

Miriam's fears and hopes spun as if on a merry-go-round, dark following on the heels of light, light turning around and chasing after dark.

She loved the ocean. She wanted to return. Miriam had never dreamed of living beneath the water—why would she have? But if she could swim and breathe like a fish, who's to say that was a bad future, all things considered? "Will you be coming with us?" The possibility that he might not became the only thing she dreaded in the fantastical future he painted.

"I can't return to the sea, I can only dream of it."

Tears sprang to Miriam's eyes. "No! Don't say that."

He gripped her hand in his. She let it remain there, feeding the connection between them. "I'm very sad that I've only met you," he said, "and now, we're going to be separated forever."

"If you're a merman, why can't you come with us?"

He rubbed his palm from the bridge of his nose to his hairline. "That's the thing," he said. "Even though the rest of my kin will be released from this curse, I'll be bound to the land forever."

"But you don't seem to like it here," she said.

"I don't have a choice."

"But if you did, you'd return to the sea."

135

"If I did, I would never have left it."

"I'll pray about all this," Miriam said.

He laughed.

"That's funny?" she asked.

"It won't do any good. It won't change anything."

Miriam disagreed.

Part VI: Dreaming of the Sea

After their talk in the park, Cole never returned to Three House Island. He turned off his mobile phone and began sleeping in one of the presidential suite's spare bedrooms. Miriam understood. He wanted to spend as much time with her as he could before she left Liberty City. He didn't tell her any more crazy stories, and there were moments when Miriam was tempted to question Gia about all the outrageous claims he'd made, but would it change anything if they were true? Would she run back to the convent? No and no.

Cole made her laugh. She helped him enjoy the simple

pleasures she discovered beyond the convent walls—pleasures he'd habitually overlooked under the constant pressure of managing Gia Ventures.

One of Miriam's favorite places was the New York Public Library on Fifth Avenue. Visits to Patience and Fortitude, the great marble lions that flanked the library entrance, replaced reverent moments she'd spent kneeling before the convent alter. After a few moments contemplation inspired by the namesakes of the noble cats, she enjoyed sitting cross-legged on the grand steps in the shadow of one of the mammoth sculptures with Cole beside her, people watching.

"I could never get bored here," she said.

Cole snorted. "Humans are vermin. The only thing they contribute to the sea is pollution!"

"You don't see their individual hopes and dreams, or the obstacles they face in achieving them." Culling examples from the library's visitors, she would describe a patron's imagined heroism and good will: The single mother attending night school to provide a better future for the infant strapped upon her back, the toddler who saved a broken-winged warbler that fell from a sugar maple tree, the harried executive who furtively shoved large bills into the hands of the homeless, and the gawky adolescent who defended his nerdy friend from a bully.

"Why do you waste your imagination on these people who care nothing for you?" Cole asked.

"They don't have to care for me in order for me to care for them."

"You're hopeless!"

"No. I'm determined. Determined not to pass on the heartache and suffering I've had to bear."

He had no response to that.

Over time, Cole's exasperated accusations faded away.

Another change: A brush of the fingertips, shoulders pressed together, a squeeze of the hand, awoke desire Miriam had declared treacherous as a child. When their evening hugs lingered, Miriam's body craved experiences she never thought she could or would. At night, when she closed her bedroom door, instead of feeling safe, she felt alone.

"He never used to come to the suite. It was all texts and telephone calls. Now, he never leaves." Gia stared openly at Miriam as if she expected the secret of Cole's unusual and constant presence to be revealed upon the young woman's face.

"We've become friends," Miriam said.

Gia's laugh was loud and guttural. "He's fallen in love with you, sweetheart."

Miriam looked away. It was Gia not Cole who leered.

"Always so reticent." Gia mused. "Perhaps that's part of the attraction." She poured herself another glass of wine. "There is an angelic quality about you. Hand me a kleenex."

Miriam reached for the lacquered box of tissues. Gia's nose ran almost constantly and her eyes were often watery since she'd stopped sending Miriam for laudanum. The circles beneath her eyes had deepened and she often paced the suite at night, suffering from insomnia. She slept more often during the day, at least she spent more time in her bedroom in the late afternoon. There had been no more rages or temper tantrums.

"That's all going to change," Gia said.

"What do you mean?" Miriam asked.

"Mer people are shallow. They only care for beautiful things and beautiful people. You'll see." Gia rubbed her chest. "This pain never goes away!"

"Can I get you some aspirin?" Miriam asked.

"Nothing is going to help until we leave." Gia refused to discuss where they were going. "All you need to know is that Cole won't be going with us."

The glint in Gia's eye hinted that dampening Miriam's spirits had lifted her own.

§§§

In spite of her exhaustion, Gia was determined to meet with as many friends as possible in the days that followed. Cole and Miriam accompanied her on the rounds. Gia never told anyone this would be the last time they would see her, but she would clasp their hands for a moment too long when she said goodbye, so that questions would fill their eyes.

Then Miriam began dreaming of the sea. At night, when she closed her eyes to sleep, her body would long for Cole. One night, she stood outside his door, listening. She gripped the door's handle with her fingers then froze.

What was she thinking? That he'd fallen in love with her?

Miriam let go of the metal as if it had burned her.

She pressed the back of her hand to her mouth. Soon, Gia would take her far away from Cole if everything they'd told her was true. She'd begun to believe that it was, because of her dreams about the sea.

The first dream began as a nightmare. Full of water snakes and sharks with sharp teeth that snapped and chased her through black sea weed that tangled liked cord around her neck. She fought to kick free, but her legs were bound, and her muscles wouldn't obey the commands of her mind. Her helpless hands flailed until she realized her legs weren't bound at all. They'd been transformed into an enormous glistening fin, like a broad paddle. She swished and kicked, tearing away from the weeds that threatened to strangle her. She whipped hard with her tail, dug deeper into the water with her hands, until the sea creatures were so far behind her that she couldn't see them anymore. Next, she shot like a missile into a dark haze. She pressed harder with her shoulders and pushed harder with her hips, propelling herself forward with an out-of-control speed. The opaque cloud became translucent. Ahead, she saw a light like the sun. She swam toward it, and that's how she woke up. Dreaming the sea was full of light.

The second dream came the next night. This time she swam hard and fast from the beginning, searching for the light. But darkness enveloped her. A song called her. It filled her with yearning and hope. It made her heart break with joy. And that's how she woke up, with tears on her cheeks.

In her third and final dream, a ghoul chained her to a reef of spiky coral, harping about this and that as it tugged and pulled the rope tighter around Miriam's chest. The never-ending cackle was a chilling sound. Miriam feared her eardrums might burst from its sharpness. Yet, in the distance, someone called her. Miriam. Miriam. Miriam. The voice drew closer. Miriam knew in her heart the person calling her would set her free, but who was it?

When she woke the next day, Miriam didn't know what to make of her dreams, but when she saw Cole, she flung her arms around him. "I'm going to miss you."

He held her tight and dug his fingers through her hair.

The final day, the final dinner, Gia, Cole, and Miriam sat in the enormous dining room once more.

"Thank you," Gia said to Cole.

He remained silent.

"Your people will be free."

"Until they need help from you again."

"Or from her." Gia pointed to Miriam.

What were they talking about?

As if she'd heard her unspoken question, Gia turned to Miriam. "Tomorrow we leave for the sea. We won't take any of this." She indicated everything around them. "We'll leave it all for Cole."

"Then it's true, everything he told me?" Miriam asked.

"What did he tell you, darling?"

Cole didn't stop Miriam as she related the outrageous things he'd said.

"I'm not surprised he left out the most important part," Gia said.

"Which is?" Miriam asked.

"The mer king came to me. His people were dying. It was a long, hard winter, and the ocean was freezing. I saved the entire kingdom."

"No, he didn't tell me that."

"No, they don't like to dwell on that part of the story. It makes them sound petty."

"Petty?" Miriam asked.

"I saved an entire kingdom and they begrudged me three sons."

Miriam sat back in her chair. This was news to her. Would she have the power to save a kingdom someday? "How did you do it?" she asked.

Gia told her.

Miriam became thoughtful. "I see."

"Enough of dwelling in the past. My days are numbered. Tomorrow we'll return to the sea, make the journey to my lair where you'll take care of me, and I'll teach you everything I know about potions and draughts, so the sea witch can live on even after I'm dead."

"Are you sure I'll be able to live and breathe underwater?" Miriam asked.

Gia pulled a vial from beneath her blouse. A fluorescent green liquid filled it. "You'll drink this, it will be painful, but it will transform you."

Miriam held out her hand.

Gia closed her hand. "Tomorrow." She left Cole and Miriam at the table.

Cole took Miriam's hand and led her through one of the french doors that led to the balcony. They stepped out into waves of heat that spilled over skyscrapers and city landmarks, creating rivulets of the paved streets far below. As the blanket of warmth enfolded Cole and Miriam, the presidential suite's chilled air seemed a world away.

They leaned against the railing. Cole fidgeted with Miriam's fingers. "It's going to be so hard to say goodbye tomorrow."

"Are you sure we'll never see one another again?" To Miriam the impossible could never be ruled out.

Cole faced her. She wore a sleeveless blouse and flared skirt.

His fingers traced the length of her arm. Tiny bumps rippled across her skin. "I've fallen in love with you," he said.

Miriam's heart stopped beating, an imperceptible pause before it began to race. "I..."

He touched his thumb to her lip. "Shhh," he said. "You don't need to say anything. Will you spend the night with me?"

Miriam closed her eyes. She wished to never live a day without Cole by her side. She craved to feel his naked skin against her own, It astounded her.

His lips grazed her forehead eliciting a pinwheel of pleasure. He pulled her to him and wrapped his arms around her. "I've never been in love before," he said. "For me it's always been and only been the sea."

For me it's always been and only been God, Miriam thought. Not the god of the church, but the god who lived in her heart, the one who always spoke when she became still enough to listen. In the absence of family, she'd transferred all her affection and trust to the invisible presence capable of sustaining and loving someone as damaged as she perceived herself to be. She had never imagined Cole, someone with a body, throwing his arms around her with yearning and desire. Her blood thundered in her ears.

She rose up on her tiptoes and whispered into Cole's ear. "Yes."

§§§

Miriam woke before dawn, Cole's arm thrown across her, his head resting in the hollow of her shoulder. She marveled that the sound and touch and taste of him had already become a part of her.

How would she leave him now?

She'd never been in love before, but love would explain the potent mix of longing, desire, joy, and regret that trammeled her heart this morning. What if she'd listened to him when he'd tried to talk her out of taking the position with Gia—the sea witch? What if she'd trusted him, from that first moment, rather than believe that he was trying to obstruct her progress in the world? They were hard questions for Miriam to ask herself, and came much too late.

Cole stirred, gripping her tighter.

Miriam trailed her finger along his forearm. He woke slowly to her tender caresses. They kissed again, pouring themselves into one another, giving the whole of their bodies to one another, promising each other: I'll never forget you. Telling each other: These moments we've shared have transformed me.

When Gia's shout came through the locked door of Miriam's bedroom, it sounded like the clang of a metal door slamming shut on an eternal dungeon. Miriam struggled to free herself from Cole's embrace, the struggle being that she didn't ever want to leave it. But she'd prayed and believed that her prayers had been answered. How foolish she'd been. The sisters had always warned her of misinterpreting the hand and word of God. What if God had been leading her to Cole and not Gia? It was hard to doubt that now. Her prayers had been answered with love, and she'd grasped for bondage. Now, if what Cole had told her was true, her soul belonged to the devil.

Miriam dressed like an automaton.

At least, she'd set Cole and the rest of his descendants free from the sea witch's curse. She tried to tell herself the sacrifice was worth it. But it was hard, when she knew Cole could have found someone else to be the sea witch's apprentice, if she'd let him, leaving Miriam free to love him.

On land.

She sighed. The snare around Miriam's heart tightened. She felt like Juliet—betrayed by the stars and fate. When she leaned over the bed, to give him one final kiss, he pulled her to him, pulling her off her feet. They rolled and tumbled in a mad embrace, their bodies cleaving to one another. Gia called again. Miriam pulled herself away, wiping her silent tears with the back of her hand. She could never have foreseen this, never have imagined it.

She ran from the room. It was all she could do.

§ § §

As soon as Miriam was out the door, Cole dressed. He threw open the curtains and stepped out onto the balcony. The heart of Liberty City beat below in the streets, at a distance in City Park, and overhead in the engine of a jet.

In a few hours, Miriam and Gia would go to the lighthouse on Three House Island. From there, they would leave him behind forever. Cole gripped onto the balcony railing. He wanted to pull it up and smash it down into the street, far below. The cold iron remained immutable, the same as his fate. He went back inside—to the room he'd shared with Miriam. It smelled of the only night they'd ever have together. It smelled of their love.

He slammed his fist into the wall. It didn't leave a trace, but hurt his knuckles. He stalked out of the room. In the dining room, he found Gia and Miriam eating breakfast. Miriam hadn't touched her food while Gia ate like a horse.

Cole gripped the back of one of the chairs. "I'll find you another apprentice," he told Gia.

"I don't want another apprentice. I've grown quite fond of Miriam. I see that you have too."

"There were other candidates."

"I like Miriam. We're leaving for the island in three hours. End of discussion."

"Gia!" Cole yelled.

"My goodness, Cole. My Miriam has really gotten under your skin."

"I love her!" he shouted.

Gia laughed. It was a hoarse, grating sound. "Love?"

Cole came round the table. He would throttle the life from her with his bare hands. Gia glared at him. "If you kill me, things won't go well for Miriam."

He halted his advance. "What are you talking about?"

"She's my apprentice. The devil will take her soul."

"Even if she never goes to the lair, never sits on the Black Thorn Throne?"

"Cole, no one's ever sat on that throne. It's impossible to find in all the rubbish. The bargain is spiritual in nature.

Miriam has accepted the bond. The devil's her master now."

Cole's face twisted in a grimace. Even though she'd told him, he still hoped there was time. "There's nothing I can do to stop this?"

"Tick-tock. Time's up." Gia fluffed her hair. She ran her forefinger along her teeth to remove a spot of lipstick. "No, not a thing."

Because of him, Miriam would suffer eternal damnation. He gazed across the table. Miriam's face was white. "I never wanted this for you," he said.

"I know," she replied.

"Miriam has had more of a choice in the matter than I ever got," Gia huffed. "I was handed over to Beulah, the sea witch before me, when I was an infant. What choice did I have? When the devil came to take her soul, he showed me no mercy, although I begged and pleaded to be free of a contract I'd never made."

"That's awful," Miriam said.

"That's the way things are. When I'm dead, you can come back on land if that's what you want to do. Spend whatever time you've got left with loverboy here."

Miriam's gaze caught Cole's eyes. "I'll come back," she

promised him.

"I'll wait for you," he said.

"All right." Gia said, "Now that that's settled, Cole, if you wish my fortune to pass onto you after my mysterious disappearance–" She waved her hands in the air. "–you'll need to go in the office and sign that stack of papers the lawyer left."

He hesitated. Was this another of her tricks?

"Go on," Gia said. "We'll join you in a moment. I need to sign them too."

He squeezed Miriam's shoulder and kissed the top of her head.

Gia rolled her eyes.

§ § §

The lighthouse still watched over the north end of Three House Island. A museum now, people swarmed up and down its spiral staircase inside and ate picnic lunches at the wooden tables outside.

Gia and Miriam would wait until nightfall to transform. The drive from the city had taken longer than usual though. There wasn't much daylight left. Gia waited in the car with the driver. Cole took Miriam by the hand and led her to the shoreline.

152

"I'm so sorry it came to this," he said.

"No, I'm sorry I didn't trust you when you warned me away. I was convinced that taking this position was what I was supposed to do. I couldn't hear anything else. I prayed, and I didn't understand the answer. I thought God had led me to Gia, but he was leading me to you. I've made an awful mess of everything." When Miriam reached up to touch his face, Cole pulled her to him.

"I'll wait for you forever," he said. "I'll come here every day, right to this spot, and watch for you."

Miriam sniffled. "I hope I can find my way back."

"Once you transform, you'll develop a sense of direction and place underwater. You'll be able to swim back here. But if you can't–" He pulled a gold ring from his finger and reached for her hand. He interlocked his fingers with hers, spreading them wide. He slipped the ring on one of her fingers and then another. It was too loose until he wedged it on her thumb. "Take this to the mer kingdom. They'll know by then that we've been released from the sea witch's curse. Tell them you're the one responsible for our freedom and that you need an escort to the lighthouse, to meet me. Tell them we're in love and that I'm waiting for you."

A sob caught in Miriam's throat. The setting sun painted the sky like a field of lavender-fuchsia-tangerine wildflowers. Tourists and visitors wandered off from the lighthouse. A cold wind invaded their final moments together.

"We can do this," Cole said. "We can remember each other and find one another again."

"I hope so," Miriam said. "I hope so."

A cough pulled them apart. Gia stood with her arms crossed.

"It will be better if I don't witness your transformation," Cole said. "It's painful and...you're going to become someone else."

Miriam's heart contracted. She couldn't believe this was the end. Her fingers slid down his arm, until at the last moment, they feathered the back of his hand. And then she felt nothing. Only the wind, tearing them apart. He trudged to the long car. The driver opened the door, and Cole disappeared behind black metal and dark windows. The driver started the engine, the car backed away.

A spike of pain carved a Cole-shaped wound in Miriam's heart. Faith in herself seeped out. She beat her chest with her fists to staunch it. Useless tears squeezed from her eyes. Nothing could change her fate now.

Miriam collapsed in the sand and pressed her palms together. She prayed for the release of a death that wouldn't come.

"Enough!" Gia removed the vial from around her neck and untwisted the silver cap. She held Miriam's chin in her hand, her nails digging into her apprentice's skin. "Open your mouth."

Miriam, with mouth clamped shut, tried to break free, but Gia was strong. "Open your mouth, girl!"

Miriam closed her eyes and released her locked jaw. Liquid dribbled over her tongue and down her throat. A stream of it ran down her chin and her neck. A wracking pain shot through her body. Miriam's legs jerked beneath her. A fiery snake inched up her spine. It felt like her feet were wrenched from her ankles. Her hips buckled and she fell back against the sand, writhing.

Gia stared the entire time.

When Miriam was spent and no more pain wracked her body, she screamed. A long black snake-like tail extended from her hips and into the waves that crashed along the beach. She looked at her hands, now gnarled and bent. Her nails looked like miniature hoofs. The ring Cole had given her dug into her bloated flesh.

"I'm going into the water now," Gia said. "We'll leave in about an hour."

Miriam whimpered on the beach, grateful that Cole hadn't remained to watch her become this hideous thing.

§§§

When she first arrived at the sea witch's lair, Miriam was aghast at the filth and the smell. She set about to clean the place. The bones were the first thing that had to go. She searched for a place to bury them. Near the base of the volcano, she found a soft spot in the sea floor where she could dig. She dug with her hands until she found some broken shells that she could use like small shovels.

"What are you doing?" Gia asked.

"They're human bones, they deserve a proper burial."

"Looks like a lot of useless work to me."

Miriam ignored her. The sea witch swam back to the lair. A few octopuses followed her. They called her Gertrude.

That night, Miriam slept deep and dreamed of Cole. The next morning she twisted his gold ring around her thumb until dark black blood oozed from the tiny cuts it made. The black fluid, more proof of her transformed and hideous state, repulsed her. But self-pity had never served her. She needed to finish the job she'd started.

Miriam grabbed the first dirty, old sack she found and filled it with the bones. For the rest of the day, she swam between the base of the volcano and the lair.

"You're making me dizzy with all this going back and forth. Can't you sit still?"

"No, Gertrude."

The sea witch flinched, but didn't say anything.

Miriam fiddled with the bag in her hands.

"Here, eat some of this." Gertrude shoved a moldy looking wooden spoon filled with a garbage-colored broth toward her. Unidentifiable bits swam in the liquid.

"What is it?" Miriam asked.

"Insects and stuff."

"No, thanks."

Gertrude slurped the contents herself. "You don't know what you're missing."

"Please, have my portion."

Gertrude shook her head. "You're a strange one."

Miriam took the last bag of bones to the massive grave. When she'd covered them with sand and dirt, and made a marker from bits of rock and shells, she prayed over them. "I'll fast for a fortnight, to help their souls find their way to heaven." It would also give her some time to find something to eat besides insect stew.

Each day, Miriam attacked another corner of the lair, another mound of rubble. One day she pricked her finger on a large black thorn. "Ouch!" Her black blood flowed from the puncture.

"What are you making a fuss about now?" Gertrude asked.

Miriam pointed to the hard black spike.

"You found the Black Thorn Throne." Gertrude pushed away more of the rubble. A high backed chair, woven from hardened black vines appeared.

"I don't like it." Miriam said. "It looks evil."

Gertrude cuffed her ears. "We're not saints." The sea witch took her seat on the throne. The seat and armrests were smooth, so the thorns didn't threaten their queen. "Next time a mer king comes, I'll sit in this. He won't be able to touch me."

Miriam hated to be reminded of Cole these days. It only made her feel like her heart was drowning.

Now that the lair was cleared, she needed something else to

occupy her mind. She returned to the borders of the sea witch's waters. Just beyond them, she saw long thin plants that swayed like tall grass. She transplanted the seaweed inside and outside the lair in artful arrangements. The plants ate the haze and the filth. The lair was unrecognizable.

On occasion, Miriam sat outside on the stoop, twisting the gold ring until her thumb bled. The sharp pinch distracted her from the pain of her breaking heart. With each day, the memories of her time with Cole faded. She no longer dreamt of him. Did he still wait for her?

Gertrude's health was weakening, but she was nowhere near death.

Miriam began to understand that forever was a long time.

§§§

"What is your name, girl?" Gertrude demanded.

The sea creature's eyes flashed with suspicion. "Do you need it to brew the potion?"

Miriam watched the exchange between Gertrude and the sea creature with curiosity.

The sea witch squinted. "I thought you were all dead."

The creature's supple body shook with mirth. The gauzy layers of her gown fluttered.

Gertrude hated to be laughed at. "Miriam!"

Miriam edged closer to the pair.

"You help this one," the sea witch said.

"Is she capable?" Now the creature pierced Miriam with her gaze. She'd said she was an oceanid.

"I'm her apprentice," Miriam explained. "She's taught me all that she she knows."

"I see." The oceanid's fathomless gaze assessed Miriam. "I want the next human I fall in love with to stay with me. I don't want him to leave." Her webbed hands buffeted the water between them. "They've all abandoned me. Every single one! I'm so lonely. I simply can't bear to lose another one."

Miriam considered the oceanid, taking in her swirls of strawberry-blonde hair, the crepey webbing that folded neatly between her fingers and toes, the thin ridges that ran the length of her arms and legs. "My name is Calypso." The unusual creature sighed. "Many a sailor has swooned in my arms, but none have proved steadfast." She pressed her hands dramatically against her chest. "I want a true love. One who will stay with me forever."

"Miriam, don't just stand there!" Gertrude picked her teeth with a bone. "Get to work."

Dreaming of the Sea

The sea witch's apprentice studied Gertrude's collections of cauldrons, buckets, and pots with a practiced eye. She chose a large, sturdy pot. Then she perused the hodgepodge of rainbow-colored vials Gertrude hid in a crooked drawer at the bottom of an old bureau rescued from a wrecked ship long ago. Miriam chose a lavender cylinder. The colorful liquids were the necessary base in every potion. Gertrude had taught Miriam how to replenish the stash by extracting the essence of sea stars, sea worms, and other brightly-shaded creatures and coral.

"I'll have to go get more lava," Miriam thought aloud.

Calypso swirled in an anxious circle.

"I won't be long." Miriam took the pot with her. She hummed as she left the sea witch's lair. Along the way, she returned the waves of the octopuses and the nods of the sea horses. Halfway to the volcano, a school of fluorescent fish swam beside her. All these interactions reminded Miriam that though she had lost Cole forever, she had gained some dear friends.

When Miriam returned, she went to work. Bringing all her knowledge to bear, she added some roots, jellied eyeballs, and a handful of seaweed to the lavender elixir. As the brew simmered she chanted an incantation Gertrude had taught her, improvised with one of her favorite hymns from her days at the convent, and added a heartfelt prayer for good measure.

The potion smelled divine. Miriam was pleased. When she handed the tiny jar to Calypso, a surge of pride swelled in her heart.

"What do I owe you?" the oceanid asked.

Miriam's tongue tied. "A bag of abalone shells?" She could string a set of decorative curtains for the lair; it would afford herself some privacy from Gertrude.

Calypso blinked her wide cerulean eyes. "Nothing else?"

Miriam shrugged. Demanding payment wasn't her forte as Gertrude ever reminded her.

When the oceanic was gone, Gertrude cuffed Miriam on the side of her head.

"Ouch! What did you do that for?"

"You've got to drive harder bargains."

"Why didn't you say something while she was still here?"

"You made the potion, you set the price. I can't interfere."

The tight band around Miriam's chest released. "You never told me that. I'll be glad to step in again."

"Not until I'm dead." Gertrude wandered toward the back of

the lair mumbling, "A bag of abalones! What kind of fool did I choose for my apprentice? She's going to ruin my fierce reputation."

§§§

Finally, years later, Gertrude lay on her deathbed.

Miriam had remained the sea witch's faithful and devoted charge, keeping the lair clean, taking over the brewing of potions, and administering soups and nourishing broth to the dying witch.

Despite all the times Gertrude had pulled Miriam's hair and kicked her in the back for every softness, Miriam had refused to change. She'd suffered as a child and had vowed long ago to never inflict the same suffering on anyone else. Better to bear the weight of sorrow and unhappiness herself than push it off onto another innocent.

"They're not so innocent," Gertrude would say.

"Who am I to judge?" Miriam would respond.

Gertrude would cuff her. "You've got a smart mouth."

Miriam didn't notice, because with every evil act she refrained from, her soul flourished.

"The devil's going to come take my soul soon," Gertrude said. "Is there anything else I can teach you?"

163

Miriam had become an expert at making the draughts for the mermaids who wanted legs and the spells for the humans who wanted fins. The octopuses and sharks had come to prefer her company over Gertrude's, and the eels followed her around, even when she'd rather they didn't. She twisted the ring, relishing its sharp sting. "How do I get back to the lighthouse after you die?"

Gertrude cackled. "You think he's waited for you all these years?"

Miriam hoped. "Yes, I do."

"When he sees you with your mottled face and greasy hair, a shapeless blob with the tail of snake, he'll fall out of love with you." Gertrude cracked her hands together with a vicious slap. "Like that."

"Then, I'll have to arrive in the dead of night, so he'll never see me like this."

"You're a strange one," Gertrude told Miriam for the thousandth time.

"I can't be anything other than who I am."

"No matter what he says, no matter what he professes, he'll always be dreaming of returning to his people, the mer kingdom, and the sea."

Miriam's heart sank. "That's true."

Gia seemed satisfied to have finally poked the vulnerable place in Miriam's heart. The sea witch closed her eyes. "The devil will be coming for me soon."

§§§

A few days later, a loud voice boomed behind Miriam. "What are you doing here?"

When she turned to answer, her tail went limp, and she drifted down among the sea weed, eyes agog.

A soot-black figure faced off with a figure in blinding, flowing white robes.

"I came to claim what's ours." The second voice, coming from the illuminated being, had the beauty of a harp.

The obsidian frog-faced creature crushed a blood-red handkerchief in his clawed fist. "The sea witch is mine."

"And her apprentice belongs to me."

"On what grounds?" the dark figure howled.

"Her heart is pure. She's committed no crimes. You can't touch her. Go now and try."

Miriam wiggled backwards as the devil advanced. He clutched at her with claw-like fingers, but an invisible force protected her. No matter how much he stretched or strained, no matter how much he twisted and turned, he couldn't catch hold of her.

"You see." The angel came from behind. "You have no claim on her. Go now, take your witch's soul and be gone!"

The devil gave Miriam such a glare, she feared she would burst into flames from the hatred in his eyes.

"Have no fear," the angel said. "God has heard your prayers, the devil can't touch you."

Miriam remained submerged in the veil of sea weed as the devil advanced to Gertrude's sick bed.

"I knew you were trouble from the moment I laid eyes on you," he said to the dying sea witch. "You! With all your whining and questions about fairness, and what is right and what is wrong." He placed one hand on Gertrude's forehead and one upon her belly. He leaned over Gertrude and latched his mouth onto hers. His face inflated like he'd swallowed a balloon. He threw his head back and licked his lips. Then he clapped his hands five times over his head.

Miriam shuddered.

"You've gotten what you came for, now go!" the angel shouted in a voice that sounded like trumpets.

The devil slinked past, shielding his eyes from the glare of the angel's bright light. When he was gone, the angel turned back to Miriam. "You've redeemed yourself. The line of the sea witch is broken." The angel held out her hand.

Miriam was ashamed to offer her gray-hide fingers and slimy palm, but the angel grasped it as if it were a babe's.

"Now, we must tend to your future," the angel said.

"My future? I want to return to land, to find the man I fell in love with."

"Then think carefully on the offer I will make."

Miriam's eyes widened, she braced herself to listen with her body, her heart, and her soul.

"You have been granted one wish."

"A wish?" Miriam was puzzled. The sisters had never told her that God dealt in wishes.

"Perhaps, you would like something that's been done to be undone?" the angel asked.

Miriam recognized the question as a clue. "Let me think." She pressed her hand against her heart. What might she want undone? This morning, she would have asked to have never taken the position as the sea witch's apprentice, but if she'd wished for that, she wouldn't be standing before an angel of God, and she'd never sacrifice this experience for anything.

The years of living with the sea witch, the separation from Cole that she hoped could now be mended, were, all of a sudden, worth it. She'd changed her fate by following her heart. By trading Gertrude's hate for love, and by not following her demands to steal from her clients the things they cherished most. The whole ordeal had strengthened and refined Miriam's nature. Perhaps she was hideous on the outside, but inside, she was beautiful. So no, to undo her bond with the sea witch, that wasn't the thing.

Then it struck her. "I can undo anything I want undone?"

"One thing," the angel responded.

Miriam shook her head. She sighed. It was a heavy choice to make. It would be a heavier one to bear. The hope of reuniting with Cole had sustained her all these long years. And yet, to know he returned to the mer kingdom, to the sea that he loved, would bring her the most joy. "I want you to return Cole's tail fins."

"You're certain this is your wish?"

"If I go to him, and my hideousness is taken from me, and we spend the rest of our lives on land, he'll be happy, by degrees. But if he could return to the sea..."

The angel waved her arm in a flourish. "So it is spoken! So

168

let it be done!"

Miriam was thrown back against the floor by concentric rings of light reverberating through and around her. Everything shook and quaked. Miriam feared the world itself would implode. She rolled over and covered her head with her hands.

Finally, the convulsions reduced to tremors and then stopped completely. Miriam peeked out from beneath her arms. The angel, the lair, even the volcano was gone. She floated in a pool of sweet, clean water. When she unfolded herself and threw out her arms to swim, a sparkle caught her attention. The gold ring Cole had given her dropped to the ocean floor! She shot forward. Her frenetic movement stirred up a cloud of sand. She groped blindly. When the silty haze settled, she couldn't find the ring. Frantic, she dug. If she couldn't have Cole, she had to have his ring! How had it slipped off? It had always been so tight around her thumb.

Sand spilled over sand, refilling every hole she made. Finally, she stopped. She needed to calm down, not bury the ring deeper in the ocean floor. Maybe if she patted the surface gently, she could feel the ring's outline. Forcing herself to be patient, Miriam pressed her palms gently against the sea floor.

After several false alarms, her chin quivered.

What had she done? Traded a future with Cole on land, so he could return to the sea and live without her.

What had possessed her?

A school of fish, an exotic rainbow of luminescence passing by, circled back to surround her. She tried to tell them that she'd lost the most precious thing she'd ever owned. The largest zebra-striped fish floated down to the sand. Two others followed. They pecked around her pale splayed fingers.

She turned her hand over. The skin on the back side was as smooth as the skin of her palms, the nails thin white crescents. That's why the ring had flown off her thumb. Her fingers were long and slim!

The fish pulled back and watched her, expectant.

She observed the sand where they'd gently nibbled. A dot of gold shone. Carefully! She reached for Cole's ring. She clutched it to her heart as the fish wiggled and swam off.

Miriam twirled in the water. Strands of long dark hair covered her eyes, but they weren't greasy strands like a sea witch's!

She pressed her palm against her cheek. The silky sensation shocked her. She rubbed her hand against her waist and slid it

170

down her body. When she reached her soft, supple scales, tiny bolts of pleasure shot through her body. She swished her opalescent tail fin effortlessly. Miriam squeezed the ring Cole had told her to take to the mer kingdom.

With no idea of how to find his people, Miriam followed the promptings of her heart. Along the way, she met a pod of dolphins, they circled around her and squeaked, dancing on their tails.

§§§

After several days, Miriam reached a gold lattice gate, guarded by mermen with spears. When she approached, they gave her strange looks and murmured about her dark hair.

She held out the ring.

They looked at her suspiciously, but agreed to take her to their king and queen.

They led her along the high sea road of the magnificent, glittering city, built from polished shells and jewels, precious metal and engraved stone. The procession thickened as more and more mer people followed behind them.

The mer king and queen sat on their shining thrones. One of the guards bowed.

"This creature claims your second son, Cole, gave her this

signet ring."

The mer queen met Miriam's gaze. Miriam recognized the hope in her eyes. "You bring news of my son?"

"He is free. Your people are free of the sea witch's debt."

"She sent you here?"

"No. Are you Cole's mother and father?"

"Yes," the mer king said.

"He gave me this ring, to show you."

The mer queen swam toward Miriam. "He gave it to you? How?"

"It's a long tale."

"We have time," the king said.

The queen waved him silent. Miriam handed her Cole's ring. His mother turned it over in her fingers. "It's his," she whispered.

"He'll be coming home. Soon, I think," Miriam said.

"Please, don't give us false hope," the mer queen said.

"Does anyone know the way to Three House Island?" Miriam asked.

"Why?"

"I must go there to meet him."

"You love him," the queen said.

"I do."

"And he loves you?"

"He did, many years ago."

The queen reached for a strand of Miriam's dark, wavy hair. The mer king and queen—everyone present except for Miriam —were golden-haired and blue-eyed.

"What kind of creature are you?" the queen asked.

"It's a long tale," Miriam said.

"So cryptic," the queen said.

"Only tired and anxious to see your son. It has been forever."

The queen's aquamarine eyes sparkled. She sang a command. Four mermen and six mermaids approached. "Escort her to Three House Island. Bring home my son."

"Thank you," Miriam said.

"We want to hear your tale," the queen said, "upon your return."

§§§

Cole woke with a jerk. Miriam.

He got out of bed and hurried to the window. The rising sun cracked the horizon. The surf was wild, the waves higher than he ever remembered seeing them.

173

He pulled on his board shorts and grabbed his board. The morning chill hit his face, his shoulders, and his chest. The water would be freezing, but the sea had him in its thrall and wouldn't release him.

He stormed down the wooden steps, crossed the grass that surrounded the pool, unlatched the gate that bordered the sand, and ran. Was that someone singing? He shaded his eyes and gazed across the water. It sounded like mer song. He hadn't heard it in decades, but now, he squinted.

The song called him home.

Return to the sea, you're free.

He dropped his board and paced along the line of the incoming tide, arms crossed, fighting the urge to throw himself in the water. What would happen to Miriam if he left Three House Island? How would she ever find him if he succumbed to the call? His entire body wanted to throw itself into the waves.

The urge to swim grew stronger.

Return to the sea, you're free.

Cole dragged his hand through his hair. He took a few steps forward. Water sloshed around his shins.

Dreaming of the Sea

Return to the sea, you're free.

Had Gia died? Was Miriam coming? He took a few more steps forward. The surf sucked at him. How long had it been since he'd been out without a board? Cole couldn't remember. He dove into an oncoming wave. His body rippled a counterpoint to the swell. His mouth creased into a smile.

Then the cramp came. He doubled over. A surge of heat ran down his spine. His legs slammed together. He fought to surface, but his legs were like deadweight. He twisted and spun in the water, and he gasped. Oxygen filled his lungs.

He stopped resisting.

Cole was breathing underwater for the first time since he'd left the sea. A shred of bright blue and orange cloth floated by. His swim trunks. He ran his hands down his abdomen and found scales. He flipped and faced his glimmering tail fin.

He was a merman again.

But how would Miriam find him now? He closed his eyes and let himself sink to the bottom. In the water, the sea witch would be hideous. Impossible to love.

Perhaps this had been Gia's final savage blow. To free him, and return him to his people, but deprive him of true love.

Cole's body heaved. He didn't have the courage to face Miriam as a bloated, greasy, and foul-smelling sea witch.

Cole released a scream that reverberated through the waters.

A school of mermaids swam toward him. Beautiful, gleaming, graceful, they greeted him. "We've come to escort you home."

The irony of his situation made it difficult to respond to the mermaid's simple statement. His sole need, to return to land and wait for Miriam, had been taken from him. On his own, his sorrow would be heavy to bear, but living among his people, joyous, happy, and full of song, it would be an impossible burden. "I can't go with you," he told the mermaid.

"You misunderstand."

Cole didn't want to explain himself, but he needed them to leave. "I've lost something, there." He pointed to the shore.

"Perhaps you lost this?" The mermaid flicked her wrist, and the mermaids parted. A single mermaid faced him, with dark brown hair that curled and twined. He'd never seen a mermaid like her.

"Cole?" she asked.

The voice felt familiar.

She swam closer. "I know I look different."

Her transformation had imparted a supernatural glow to the simple beauty of her human form.

"Miriam?" He pulled her to him. "Miriam! Miriam!" Cole ran his fingers through her hair. Their tail fins twined into one. He pressed his hands against the sides of her face and gazed into her eyes. "I was so afraid I'd lost you forever."

She told him what had happened when the sea witch died.

"Then, your soul is your own?"

"Yes."

"But will you be happy living in the sea?" he asked.

The mermaids tittered.

Miriam blushed. "This is the life I've always dreamed of, and it has finally found me."

"You were right," he said.

"What do you mean?"

Cole's eyes blazed. "You followed your heart."

"I did."

"I will never let you go again," he promised.

When his lips found hers, the sonic vibration of their reunion reverberated for miles.

A multitude of sea creatures—dolphins, glow fishes,

seahorses, and sea turtles among them—responded. They escorted Miriam and Cole home through the deep silky waters.

Author's Note

When I read the original version of the "The Little Mermaid",
I was surprised with its spiritual emphasis. None of the movie
remakes or retellings I'd read conveyed the original tale's
underlying theme: Mermaids don't have souls and the little
mermaid wanted one. Rather profound. But it left me with a
dilemma. I have two goals for each *Once Upon a Time Today*
novella. The first is to update the story with characters and
setting, the second is to remain true to the original fairy tale's
essence while providing some kind of twist.

I realized if I remained true to the essence of "The Little

Mermaid", I'd be grappling with spiritual themes. I chose to go ahead and twist the original tale by having a mortal at risk of losing her immortal soul.

Although the sea witch is a critical figure in the original tale, she doesn't get a lot of stage time. I'd read *Wicked* years ago and loved the spin on the Wicked Witch of the West, so I decided to focus my retelling on the witch as well. One fun detail: We see the "original" little mermaid come to the sea witch's lair and have quite an impact on the sea witch's apprentice in *Dreaming of the Sea*.

When it came to setting, I decided to make use of the convent that served as an important place in the original tale. Out of that decision, Miriam was born. Determined, but also dreamy, her journey in the story is quite spectacular.

Thank You

I appreciate you spending your valuable time reading *Dreaming of the Sea*. If you'd like to share the story with other readers, please tell a friend, or post a review on any book-ish site.

I'd also like to invite you to sign up for my newsletter: http://eepurl.com/wWKUj. It's quirky—like me:D—and I confess, it comes out sporadically, but I send a variety of things, including some (hopefully) pleasant surprises along with updates on all my new releases.

Sincerely,

Acknowledgment

Thank you

Brandy Scofield

Jimena Novaro

Lynn Perry

Tanya Johnson

For Being Early Readers

First Chapter of Beautiful

Beautiful

Mirabella rolled off her father's back.

She giggled and snorted as she caught herself with her hands and launched onto her short, slender legs.

Her daddy reared up on his knees, twisted, and waved his arms over his head. "GRROWR!"

Seven-year-old Mibi dashed into the kitchen, screaming, "You can't catch me, Daddy!"

Her daddy collapsed on the floor. "Not even gonna try."

Kerrin slid from the sofa to cross her husband's body with hers. Lying stomach to stomach, she propped herself on her elbows, hands splayed over her eyes, acting as the lookout for their daughter's return.

When Mibi peeked out from the kitchen, Kerrin closed the space between her fingers. "I can't see you!"

Bare feet slapped the hardwood floor. When they became a muffled shuffle, Kerrin braced herself. Mibi threw her body against her parents—an exuberant torpedo of arms, legs, and laughter. Her daughter's thick, waist-length hair spilled over Kerrin's face as their three bodies collapsed into a flattened mass.

Mibi's arms clutched her mother's neck in a stranglehold. "Tell me the *beauty beauty* story."

"Are you sure that's the one you want tonight?"

Mibi let go of her mother's neck and patted her cheeks. "Yes!"

Almost every night Kerrin told her daughter a fairy tale. The bonding ritual had begun a few years ago on a trip. They'd forgotten to pack Mirabella's favorite bedtime stories, and Kerrin had improvised with a fairy tale, drawing symbolism from her personal history. The experiment had been such a success, they'd repeated it over and over.

Kerrin had discovered a creative way to pass meaningful lessons from her life on to her daughter, and Mibi cherished the opportunity to reshape the tale each time it was told by asking questions and interjecting her own opinions and commentary.

As Kerrin struggled to get up, her daughter cleaved to her side—an extension of her mother's body. Her husband offered them a hand. When they were steady on their feet, he brushed his wife's cheek with his lips and ran his hand over his daughter's hair.

That simple gesture reminded Kerrin why *beauty beauty* had become one of her favorite fairy tales to tell, in spite of its inherent challenges.

Kerrin transferred Mibi to her husband. When their daughter was secure in his arms, with her head nestled against his neck, they walked down the hall to Mibi's bedroom.

Daddy tucked Mibi in, and then turned off the overhead light and waved goodnight.

Kerrin flicked on the small lamp on the nightstand, and

settled on the bed next to her daughter.

Mibi took hold of her mother's hand.

§§§

"Once upon a time there was a girl who believed in beauty," Kerrin began, "and there wasn't an aspect of beauty that she couldn't appreciate."

"Did she have a Daddy?" Mibi asked.

"No, but she had a fairy godmother."

"What was the fairy godmother's name?"

"Hannah."

"What about her mother?"

"The girl's mother was possessed by a dark enchantment."

"What was her name?"

"Emery."

Mibi giggled. "That's Gramma's name."

"Yes, it is."

"Why did the girl like beauty so much?"

"Because she realized it was everywhere, and no matter how many things she lost, or how many things were taken away from her, or even how many things she'd never had in the first place, beauty was always available."

"Like a purple flower that grows in a broken sidewalk," Mibi said.

"A black panther stalking through the jungle," Kerrin imagined zooming in on the big cat with a lens.

"The snow before it gets dirty and melts."

"A rainbow after the storm has passed."

"My ballet shoes."

"My daughter."

Mibi beamed.

No image could compete with that smile in Kerrin's heart.

Before the birth of her daughter, Kerrin had feared years spent behind a camera might have stunted any maternal instinct she possessed. If anything, her observant eye increased her ability to tune in to Mibi's spirited personality.

§§§

Kerrin Mayham avoided eye contact with the other guests as she studied the room. It was her nature to balance and weigh every element: color; furnishings; space. Since she could remember, she assessed each detail of any new physical environment. Her eye sought asymmetry and dissonance as much as order and balance, measuring light and angles to frame the perfect shot in her mind.

"Kerrin."

Being interrupted before she settled the shot made her anxious. That single decision, highly personal, made her feel secure, no matter where she was or who she was with. It had since she'd started playing her private game, decades ago.

She forced herself to smile at the president of the Golden Pinnacle guild and the party's host. "Frank."

"Are you enjoying yourself?" he asked.

"It's an honor to be here."

He stopped one of the waitresses roving by with platters of champagne flutes, and handed Kerrin a glass. "Marais-Leroux-Delair."

She took a sip. "It's wonderful."

"Only the best to celebrate the Golden Pinnacle nominees. Are you nervous about the awards show tomorrow night?"

"Of course."

"Don't be," Frank said.

"Are you privy to inside information?"

Probably everyone in the room had or would ask him that question tonight. A giggle escaped her lips. It was an embarrassing, nervous sound. She raised her glass and drained the remains. Swilling expensive champagne lacked grace, but as one of the top five female directors on the indie film circuit, she'd learned it was better to break rules with conviction. Determination set trends.

She flagged down the next waitress herself and handed Frank a glass.

"I know A Scorched Heart is a masterpiece." He tilted his head. "It was your vision that made every frame of that film a work of art."

Was he telling her that she'd won? It was hard to say. Maybe he fawned over all the nominees.

She raised her glass in a toast anyway. "Thank you."

He sidled up to her, glancing around the room—a king surveying his subjects. "Benji!" Frank waved over a thirty-something white guy with black ear studs and gnarly eyebrows. "Have you met Kerrin Mayham?"

The younger man shook her hand.

"Benji reps James Fellowes. You know him? Young guy, light hair, dark eyes, straight eyebrows." Frank's eyes twinkled.

She wondered if he thought Benji's eyebrows were gnarly too, but she couldn't place James Fellowes. But then all the hot actors in Glitter City looked like gods descended.

"Another young Adonis?" Kerrin asked.

"Yeah, him," Benji said.

"The studio's optioned this script," Frank continued, speaking to both of them. "Demion Glass. It's about a guy possessed by demons."

Horror wasn't Kerrin's thing. "I haven't heard of it." Her mind roamed. She swiveled her head in both directions. How was it possible there wasn't a single waitress in sight?

"We're going to offer it to the winner," Frank said.

"Actor of the Year?" she asked.

"Nah," Frank said, "Director of the Year."

He was talking to her.

"Have you ever worked with a studio budget, Kerrin?"

"No, it's always been indie for me."

"You've never really made a movie until you've worked with the big boys," Benji said.

She would not knee him in the groin.

Frank crossed his arms. "I came up on the indie circuit. Shoestring budgets are the best way to learn the nuts and bolts."

Benji wiped visible sweat from his brow with a cocktail napkin.

Frank patted him on the back. He took Kerrin's arm and led

her away. "There's a few more people I'd like you to meet tonight."

§§§

"So finding beauty helped the girl?" Mibi asked.

"Yes, it did. Whenever she was lonely or disappointed, she would go in search of the most beautiful thing she could find that day. When she found it, her troubles slipped away."

"How did she know when she found it?"

"Her heart would feel like it could fly."

"I don't have any troubles."

Kerrin smiled at her daughter's failure to recall the minor complaints she'd voiced earlier that evening. "Someday you might." Everyone did. However, gazing at her daughter, Kerrin intuitively understood the challenges in Mibi's life would be far different than the ones she'd faced. She doubted there would be a Tom in her future. With Mibi's father so involved in his daughter's life, she wouldn't need a father figure. The thought lightened Kerrin's heart. Tom had been a desperate, reckless mistake. Although not her only one.

"I'm going to be the only person on the planet who doesn't have any troubles!" Mibi brought Kerrin back from her musings.

"But if you ever do—"

"Mommy, I'll remember to look for something beautiful."

§§§

Sherri Winestine, the aging, yet sleek agent for Bruce Rik, was the next person Frank introduced Kerrin to. He definitely had an agenda.

Her heart floated. Would the rest of the nominees receive similar treatment before the night was over, or had Frank singled her out?

A frumpy woman approached with a young god in tow. Kerrin blinked. He really could be Adonis wearing a faded green t-shirt, worn chinos, and rubber flip-flops. Had to be an actor. The raw talent that generated every light in Glitter City, actors got away with everything. Inappropriate attire was the least of the social crimes they were forgiven.

Kerrin glanced up at the recessed light fixtures. A ricochet of shadow?

No, the closer he got the better he looked.

So scrubbed and fresh. The fingers of her right hand curled. God, she needed her camcorder.

"Frank!" the frumpy woman shouted.

The host held out both his arms. The woman almost bowled

194

him over with her enthusiasm for his embrace. He closed his eyes and patted her back.

The woman yanked on Adonis' hand as if he were her five-year-old son. "Here he is. The one I told you about. Anthony Zorr." She made an impressive maneuver, exiting the close embrace with Frank to shove her beautiful find in his face.

Sherri waved and wandered off.

Anthony grinned.

Dawn shimmered across a rising tide.

Kerrin lost track of the conversation. All she saw were those cheekbones, those masculine bow lips, and that stance—not bloated and beefy, just taut. And tan. He glistened. Standing with his hands jammed into his pockets, he gave off an air of bashfulness.

Where had he come from?

She re-tuned to the conversation. Ah, just off the bus, and all the way from the cornfields in Iowa. He wouldn't stay untouched for much longer. Kerrin wanted him—she didn't know for which film, and she didn't care. She just wanted him in front of her camera, filling frame after frame with that natural boyish exuberance at the edge of becoming a man.

"How old are you?" Kerrin asked.

Anthony, the woman with him, and Frank looked at her as if something living had gotten caught between her teeth.

"Ma'am?"

He had called her ma'am. She couldn't decide whether it was endearing or insulting. Maybe a little of both.

Kerrin pressed on. There were at least four other directors in this room who would lure him, hook him, steal him away from her. She wasn't going to let them. "My name is Kerrin Mayham."

He took her proffered hand. "Right on."

His handshake was firm, dry. The promise of that simple physical exchange charged her body.

"Kerrin Mayham!" the frumpy woman blared.

All the heads in the room turned in their direction. Kerrin flattened her hand against her thigh to resist the reflex to cover her ear.

Oblivious to the foghorn effect of her voice, the woman continued. "I'm such a fan of yours! I've seen every single film you've ever made. Anthony is twenty-four. He has a great look, don't you think?"

"Yes," Kerrin said.

"And he's not just a pretty face. He's won awards."

She assumed for acting. "That's great," Kerrin said.

"Anthony, Kerrin's one of the five directors nominated for the Director of the Year," Frank said.

"Nice to meet you, ma'am."

There it was again. That ma'am.

"Please, call me Kerrin."

"Have you met Marni Lamb?" Frank asked. "She's an agent with Colossal Talent."

The frumpy woman wedged herself between Kerrin and Frank. "We've met now."

Kerrin was again impressed with the physical agility of someone so rectangular. Anthony spread his legs and settled his arms in reverse fig leaf. Kerrin imagined camera angles. Vivid expression. Anthony blessed her with another shy smile.

Marni squeezed Kerrin's arm with two hands. "Anthony's going to make a huge splash in Glitter City," she said. "First film—he'll be a star. I know these things."

Kerrin couldn't disagree.

"What do you think, Frank?" Marni pointed to her client. "Is he Demion Glass or what?"

Frank slid his index finger along his eyebrow. "It's possible. Absolutely, possible. Bring him by to meet Glenda at the end of the week?"

"You want to wait to the end of the week? Another studio might snap him up tomorrow."

She actually chucked Anthony under the chin, and he allowed her to do so. Midwest polite?

"It's going to be crazy the next few days," Frank said.

Marni waved her hand. "I know. I know. It always is when the Pinnacle winners are announced. But you don't want to let this one slip away, do you? Glenda could spare five minutes for me."

"Tell her I told you to call her and squeeze him in as soon as possible. How's that?"

"Oh, that's perfect." Marni squeezed her hands into baby-like fists and bounced them up and down. "You won't regret it."

She gave Frank another bear hug and squeezed Kerrin with equal enthusiasm before dragging Anthony away.

"That's Marni," Frank said. "She'll hit all the studio heads tonight." He stopped one of the waitresses, took two glasses from her tray, and offered one to Kerrin.

She didn't want any more champagne.

Watching Anthony's back, all Kerrin yearned for was her

camera.

§§§

"One day the girl met the most beautiful boy in the world," Kerrin said.

"Mommy, boys aren't beautiful."

She ruffled her daughter's hair. "You might change your mind about that one day."

Mibi stuck her index finger in her mouth and pretended to gag.

"If you'd seen this boy, you would have thought he was beautiful too."

"What color were his eyes?"

"The color of the ocean on a sunny day."

"What color was his hair?"

"Gold like a wheat field."

"Did the girl fall in love with the boy?"

No matter how many times Kerrin told her daughter *beauty beauty*, Mibi always asked *that* question. She returned her daughter's mischievous grin. Mibi was too young for an overt discussion on the ins and outs of animal magnetism. Kerrin just hoped the truth in her embellished tale would seep into

199

her daughter's subconscious, a protective seed that would blossom if it was ever needed.

About the Author

Heidi Garrett is the author of the *Daughter of Light* fantasy trilogy about a young half-faerie, half-mortal searching for her place in the Whole.

She's also the author of *Once Upon a Time Today*, a collection of modern fairy tale retellings for adults who have already left home. *The Magic Cupcake* series is paranormal romance trilogy she writes with Billie Limpin.

Heidi was born in Texas, and attempted to reside in as many cities in that state as possible. She made it to Houston, Lubbock, Austin, and El Paso. After spending a decade in southern California, she now lives in Eastern Washington state with her husband, their two cats, her laptop, and her Kindle. Being from the South, she often contemplates the magic of snow.

You can find Heidi on her blog.